About the Author

JT Torres is an assistant teaching professor of English at Quinnipiac University. His forthcoming book with University Press of Florida, entitled *Situated Narratives and Sacred Dance: Performing the Entangled Histories of Cuba and West Africa*, explores the performance of identity in the ritual ceremonies of Arará communities in Cuba. *Taking Flight* is his debut fiction work.

Taking Flight

JT TORRES

Fairlight Books

First published by Fairlight Books 2021

Fairlight Books
Summertown Pavilion, 18–24 Middle Way, Oxford, OX2 7LG

Copyright © JT Torres 2021

A CIP catalogue record for this book is available from the
British Library

1 2 3 4 5 6 7 8 9 10

ISBN 978-1-912054-09-1

www.fairlightbooks.com

Printed and bound in Great Britain by Clays Ltd.

Designed by Sara Wood

Illustrated by Sam Kalda
www.folioart.co.uk

For Coraida Hermana Castaño Badía, la gran ilusionista (1920–2012)

I

Nana appeared by my bed, staring at me with vacant eyes that I felt responsible for filling. The pre-dawn moonlight sliced by the blinds iced her skin a soft blue. She was wearing the red shawl I bought for her one Christmas, with the black double-breasted lapel pointed up above her ears, a gothic collar, all of it making her look like a Bela Lugosi mistress. The shawl cloaked her body, the trim draping onto the floor. She could have been floating, but that would have been too predictable. I had grown used to Nana's midnight presence out here in Alaska. Since I moved to Anchorage, she's been the only person from my family to visit.

'How do you do it?' I asked and kicked off the sheets that stuck to my skin, what skin I had left. A quarter of my body had become invisible. That, at least, was *normal*. I had been disappearing off and on for the past couple of years, like a bulb about to burn out for good. What I wasn't used to was the numbness. Now, when an arm vanished, so did the feeling in my fingers, hand, and everything up to where my arm became solid. I became numb, nothing.

'Viola,' I said and held up my invisible arm. It had the weight of a shadow.

Nana smiled, watching me with those eyes that searched for secrets I didn't know I kept. I remembered my mother asking her questions about her life, as if the questions, if answered correctly, could cure dementia. Nana would look at me as she did now. All mystery, like a story without an ending. The details always changing. Not even the color of Nana's eyes could be determined with any certainty. Warm hazel, but Nana always swore they were green.

I climbed out of bed and found my wallet, removing my Alaska driver's license with my one visible hand. Using the snow-gray light from the window, I pointed to my height and showed Nana: 5'4".

'I've lost more than half a foot,' I said. 'I don't know how to stop the illusion.'

Nana walked past me and stared out the window. Blocks of boxy white buildings surrounded my apartment. I wondered what Nana thought of my living in Anchorage. She would have never visited Alaska alive. The cold was too much for her Cuban blood, she'd said once.

'I tried not worrying when my hair thinned and I went bald before I left Florida,' I said. 'My Florida license listed me as 6'1". Moving somewhere cold was supposed to reverse the spell. Soon, the wind will carry me away.'

All she did was tap her finger against the frosted window.

I stood next to her, trying to find what captured her interest. Three stories below streetlights glowed yellow orbs, casting a hazed radiance on the snow-covered sidewalk. Sweat dripped down my legs.

She filled my room with the scent of nostalgia.

'Will you answer me this time?' I asked.

Of course she wouldn't. She had warned me enough times not to cast a spell I couldn't manage. Not to use illusion against the self, not to disguise reality to the point of deception. Sometimes, when she was alive and I asked her for help, she'd only tell me the answer in Spanish. That way, she said, I'd either learn illusion or her language. Everything was always a game, including her own life. Her standing at my window in my apartment became a puzzle I had to assemble. After all, she had been dead for longer than a year.

Still, I wanted her to say something. Anything. Say she needed to find my mother. Say she felt alone. Call me Tito-my-love. All I needed was her voice.

My hands gripped the smooth velvet lining of her shawl, a perfect gift. Somehow, I must have known she'd wear it in the afterlife. I wanted to tell her this, tell her that I'd improved my magic, tell her I was learning. I wanted to ask her to stay a little longer this time. I wanted to tell her that Mom was getting worse, losing her memory, too, and saying things that didn't make much sense. That childish feeling of surprise, of joy at the world and all its ineffable, effervescent wonders, hardened like a callused heel at my anxiety, and instead I felt something else. Expectation. Disappointment. I knew what was next. Nana did it all the time. She disappeared.

*

When I was around five years old, my mother bought a parakeet for Nana. But Nana wouldn't even look at the fluttering topaz bird inside the silver-wired cage. 'I don't want it,' she said.

Nana never wanted a pet, so it worried my mother whether she'd actually take care of one. With that worry in mind, she decided on a more 'disposable' animal. Pets are measured on some kind of life-value scale. Parents never start kids off, for example, with a dog, which is of the 'best friend' category. They get their potentially irresponsible children an ant-farm, a goldfish, or a hamster, something from the pet-practice-squad.

Much later, when I was ten, I'd won a plastic-bagged goldfish from the Miami Fair. I named the goldfish Goldie. But that was all I did.

After two days, I found him belly-up in his plastic bag. I never had time to get him a bowl. And to be honest, I never even had time to name him. I just came up with 'Goldie' for the sake of the story. After my mother flushed Goldie down the toilet, though, I became heartbroken. I went around saying, 'Goldie's dead because I'm an accident!'

A parakeet is also of the disposable variety of pets.

This was when we lived in Miami, when my mother was all Nana had. It had been several years since Nana came to America from Cuba, but she never assimilated. She referred to herself as an exile. 'I will never be a citizen in another country again,' she would protest. She didn't make any friends. She never kept a job longer than a month, mostly because she bragged that she was not an American citizen, even though she actually was. And after my grandfather died, I was told, Nana needed someone to look after her.

This presented a problem for a love-starved child.

I was younger than my sister, a child for whom they actually planned. They had no plans for me, I've been told, making me an accident and the youngest. As such, it was kind of my job to have all my mother's attention. I worked hard to be an accident, which, it turns out, is the only thing I'm good at.

In my earliest memories of my relationship with Nana, I felt directly threatened by her. I also hoped the parakeet idea would work.

'I gave birth to you,' Nana reminded my mother.

'And I gave birth to Tito,' my mother reminded her.

'I gave you your name: Penny.'

'I have a child to take care of already.'

My mother claimed that until school started, she would be very busy watching me and working for my father. I remember my mother holding me against her chest while she said this. I remember how her grip tightened, squeezed fear into my thigh. While I might not have been able to fathom the gravity of their conversation, I do remember the discomfort of her grasp, and of Nana's sharp stare, at both me and my mother.

'He's too big for you to carry him,' Nana said. 'Put him down.'

'You used to carry me home from school when I was eight, embarrassing me in front of my friends and teachers. You didn't listen to Dada when he told you to put me down.'

'That was in Cuba,' Nana said. 'Things are different in America.'

My mother always remarked how Nana was stubborn as a rock. Sometime during her forties, Nana had a dentist remove all of her teeth because she didn't want to pay for a filling. My mother used to tell everyone that Nana's 'stubbornness is greater than pain'. At the time, I was scared of Nana, scared that she was mad at me for something I didn't understand. When she talked about me to my mother, her voice cut. 'I bet *he* loves spending the day with you all the time,' she said once. She walked around in platform shoes that made her taller than my mother, and my father for that matter. Each step she took had the thunderous quality of crashing waves.

I remember Nana as the savage queen of a verdant jungle. She lived in an apartment with brown walls, mulch-colored furniture, and rows of plants. Dirt and several petals spilled from flowerpots.

It was where an exile would live.

'You don't try to make friends here,' my mother finally said and walked towards the front door.

'My friends are in Cuba.' Nana stomped a foot down. The earth trembled. The parakeet flew to the cage's ceiling. The plants rocked in their pots, and a few white petals floated to the floor. My mother squeezed me, the side of her breast pushing into my stomach.

I'd never been to Cuba, where Nana was born. Nana had returned a number of times. Not only did she meet my grandfather in Cuba, but she also took my mom once when she was a child. Something, though, always brought Nana back to America. I imagined Cuba looked just like Florida, but with mountains. Here in Florida, Nana was the only mountain.

'You've lived in Miami for twenty years now!'

My mother put me down and we walked to the car. As she loaded me in my car seat, I looked towards the apartment and saw Nana leaning on the railing, watching us. The shadow of her figure split the sun's light, and from inside the car I could feel her loneliness.

My mother wouldn't let the parakeet starve, so once a week she and I would go to Nana's apartment to feed him and clean his cage. Since getting her a pet, my mother began spending *more* time with Nana.

*

Nana named the parakeet Pepe. But that was all she did.

The first 'Pepe' Nana owned was lime green with chalk-blue circles around his eyes. When he lifted his white-tipped wings, he revealed yellow shadows on each side of his body. During our visits I'd stare through the thin wires of the cage and watch the bird bolt from corner to corner. I so badly wanted to hold Pepe but feared Nana would yell at me to put him down.

Once, when I was certain my mother and Nana were having coffee in the kitchen, out of view of the living room where the cage was, I slid my pinky through the individual wires and nudged Pepe. His feathers felt firm but flimsy, like they'd dissolve in the wind but continue to float as individual fibers and brittle bones. He had a certain edge, despite how fragile he appeared to be. When I nudged him a second time, he turned around and pecked me. I hollered, and when I noticed a drop of blood I cried. My mother came running and scooped me into her arms. She took me into the kitchen and held a tissue over my injured pinky. Nana stared at me with a look as sharp as Pepe's beak, a look that I would later learn to identify as judgment. She said, 'Don't poke around where you don't belong.'

At five, I was too young to have a pet of my own. Even a goldfish would have been too much responsibility. Besides, my father disliked animals. He claimed they were unruly. In my parents' home, file cabinets lined the living-room walls and tax documents occupied the dining-room table. My bedroom dresser had two drawers reserved for clients' cash receipts.

I craved disorder. I spent my time at home exploring the fenced-in backyard, trying to catch lizards. Every time I'd snare one by its tail, the lizard would snap its body free. Pepe, a live animal in Nana's wild apartment, had been an unthinkable possibility. This intrigue was heightened by my fear of both him and her. While I do remember not wanting to visit Nana, I also remember my desire to hold Pepe in my own hands. I wanted to possess what made Nana wild. Of course, I didn't have a choice whether or not we visited, but I felt like I belonged in her apartment. It was where an accident would live.

When my mother and I showed up one week, several days after my pinky had healed, we found Nana crying on the sandstone-patterned sofa. Pepe was lying on his side on the wicker coffee table, his eyes closed and body motionless.

'Oh my God,' my mother said and ran to Nana. She sat next to her and pulled Nana's face into the space between her neck and shoulder, shielding her eyes.

This was ridiculous. For one, Nana had obviously already seen that Pepe was dead. Second, I was the child here. No one shielded my eyes. Even a few years later, when Goldie died, my parents didn't at all worry about how death affected me. Apparently, a parakeet's life is at least three points higher on the life-value scale than a goldfish. Or a son.

I stood by the front door. Nana's apartment felt damp and cold. The air chilled my skin's sweat. The apartment seemed to have become a much more dangerous place since the last visit. I could now sense predators lurking in the plants, hunting me from the hallway. Growing up in Florida, I learned from school fieldtrips to the Everglades to stand still if facing a black bear, run in zigzags if chased by an alligator, and avoid eye contact with a panther. What they never taught us was how to flee a wild grandmother.

'He stopped moving after I bathed him,' Nana said, sobbing with her hands in her lap, her fingers locked, and her face buried in my mother's neck.

'You bathed him?' The compassion in my mother's voice gave way to anger. 'You don't bathe birds.'

'He smelled bad.'

'He's dead.'

My mother stood up from the sofa and went into the kitchen. She came back with a roll of paper towels and used them to wrap Pepe like a bird mummy. Then she carried him back into the kitchen. Nana's eyes were red and swollen. She looked much more vulnerable than I'd ever seen her. Without her false teeth to prop up her lips, her mouth drooped onto her chin. She looked at me and I felt her sadness. As a child, I did not know what that feeling was, but it felt familiar, like I was supposed to know it.

'I miss hearing him chirp,' she said. 'He almost learned to say "Big Mama's here".' The way she pitched her voice so that it squeaked like Pepe's made me smile. My smile made Nana smile.

'You don't bathe birds, Mom. I mean, that's common sense.'

'You always scold me like I'm a child.'

My mother walked back into the living room with a long sigh, creating her own gust of wind. She told Nana to put on her shoes. 'I can't leave you alone now.'

Nana's puffy eyes and the large swooping curls of her hair softened her look. I wanted to be next to her, to feel this new softness. My mother brought her with us back to our house, where she watched TV in the living room while my mother punched tax codes into the computer in her office. I had crawled on an empty shelf in one of the metal storage cabinets in the hallway, and from there spied on Nana. She seemed oblivious to the images flashing across the TV screen. Whenever the sound of laughter came from the speakers, she kept a stern expression, silent. All I could think about was Pepe. Was his death painful? What had my mother done with his body? Did Nana *kill* him? Would Nana kill *me*? Pepe wasn't safe in a cage; was I safe in a cabinet?

When my mother came out of her office and told Nana she had to take her home, Nana started crying.

'What's wrong with your home?' my mother said in a voice strained by impatience and pity. While my mother inherited Nana's sternness, she lacked her powerful presence. There were times when my mother and I shared a room and I could not sense her. I could feel Nana, though, at opposite ends of Miami.

'I miss him.'

'Well, Mom, you can't bathe birds.'

'I miss your father,' Nana snapped, as if irritated that my mother didn't understand her the first time. My grandfather died in Cuba before I was born. It was entertaining to witness these moments in which my mother became the child. So often did my mother snap at me for not knowing certain things, like how to pour my own orange juice without spilling it.

My mother sat with Nana and hugged her so their heads rested together. They spoke to each other in Spanish, a language I did not know. I rarely heard my mother speak Spanish, but when she did, she became someone else entirely. Her voice became urgent, powerful. I finally crawled out of the cabinet. There was no place for me in the moment shared between my mother and Nana. Despite how badly I wanted to join them, I ran to the bathroom.

Later, we took Nana to the pet store and bought her another parakeet, Pepe II.

The new Pepe looked almost identical to the old one, save for two apple-red pinstripes on either side of his tail. Also, Pepe II's eyes seemed wider, more alert, as if he sensed his predecessor's demise. I doubt, though, that parakeets have clairvoyant abilities.

*

About a month later, I overheard my mother telling my father that Nana drowned Pepe II. They were speaking in my father's office, a room I wasn't allowed to enter, mostly because of the whole me-being-an-accident thing.

His office had the house's largest TV set, two computers, a printer, and a wrap-around desk. One time, I snuck into his office and decided it would be a good idea to play with all the wires under his desk. When my father couldn't turn anything on, he yelled to my mother, 'Gee, honey, can you remind that frolicking son of yours to please avoid my office?' (Except he used *other* words.)

From the doorway, I watched as my father sat in the center of the room, enclosed by a desk that seemed to extend out from his body. A computer screen cast a cold blue glow on his wide-frame glasses and shiny forehead. He had paper stands and two calculators arranged all within arm's reach. The desk appeared to be a spaceship with a 360-degree control panel, so naturally I wanted to play on it, sit in his chair, and imagine cruising through space, but doing so probably would have led to *my* drowning. *I just tried bathing him*, I imagined my father saying, feigning innocence.

'You think she's doing it on purpose?' my father asked. He poked at his calculator with one rigid finger that made him look like a captain. *Blast off!*

My mother leaned against the wall adjacent to the door. This was really the only space where one could fit in my father's office if not in the captain's seat. 'Why would she do it on purpose?'

'Does she even like birds?'

My mother looked over at me and her eyes became heavy. Something about her stare weighed on me, so I did my best to stand firm and carry it. She reached out and ran her fingers through my hair.

'It is hereditary,' my mother said.

'That doesn't mean she has it.' My father's voice seemed to follow the rhythm of the calculator's taps and clicks. Everything about him remained in perfect order.

'My aunt died asking for relatives who'd passed away years prior. Before my grandfather's last heart attack, he went around the house smashing picture frames and toppling furniture because he didn't know where he was.'

While they spoke, I thought of Pepe, motionless on the table, and Nana's puffy eyes and melting face. Even though I didn't understand what my parents were talking about, I realized it was something Nana and I both shared – me an accident and her an exile.

My mother led me out of his office and as we walked into the living room, she began to cry. Titi, my sister, who had been watching TV on the couch, asked what was wrong. Since she was eleven, she didn't have to join us on our trips to Nana's. In our family, eleven was the age that qualified one to be left alone at home.

'We can't find a bird Nana actually likes,' my mother said.

'Can we have a bird?' Titi asked. She tugged our mother's hand, as if she knew exactly where to get one. Titi spoke with a maturity beyond her age. Once, when she got in trouble for something at school, I watched her on the phone with the principal, pretending she was our mother. It worked!

'You know your father doesn't like animals.'

I sensed in my mother a need to protect me from something, and I understood the only way she could do that was by not telling me the truth, as if the truth was what I needed protection from.

*

Once again we were on the way to the pet store, my mother driving with Nana sitting up front and me strapped in the backseat. We had just left a McDonald's drive-thru. The a/c roared but could not cool the hot car. My hands sweat onto my hamburger. All around us, the sun glared off metal, burning the edges of my memory.

Nana, washed out by the sun, sipped her iced tea and then looked helplessly at my mother, her eyes all big and confused, her mouth frowning. She said, 'Sometimes, everything tastes like cats.'

'Cats?' my mother asked, glancing at Nana while stopped at a light.

'The cats I ate,' Nana said. 'When we got to America and didn't have money, your father would find cats on the street for us to eat.'

'We never ate cats.'

Nana turned and looked at me. 'To this day it breaks my heart to see a stray cat,' she said in a dramatic tone, like she was being filmed.

'No, Mom,' my mother sighed. 'That was a story your sister used to tell us. She used to say that after the revolution there wasn't any food *in Cuba*, so people started eating cats or whatever.'

Nana shot her eyes back at my mother. 'You think I'm making that up? I remember it clear as it was yesterday! Your father would have it skinned by a neighbor, then come home and roast it. It tasted like this iced tea, rough and papery.' There was desperation in her voice, something I couldn't understand but still felt.

'Dad was friends with someone who ran a chicken farm,' my mother said. The entire time she kept driving, both hands locked on the wheel. She spoke firmly and directly, like she did with her clients, like Nana just needed to tidy up on some taxes. 'You used to say all the time how you were sick of eating chicken because that's all you had.'

Nana shrugged and looked out the window.

I peeked into the greasy happy meal box. A few French fries remained, those that spilled from their paper container. I imagined them being made of cat meat – cat fingers! – and wondered if I could continue eating. I nibbled on one but couldn't get past the idea. Without being certain she was telling the truth, I felt sorry for Nana.

At the pet store, my mother sought an attendant while Nana and I walked to the glass cage of parakeets. Feather bolts of sapphire and lime dashed in every direction. Colorful ribbons blurred with soft palpitations of air as the birds flapped their wings. Nana leaned on my shoulder and lowered her head. The tip of her nose touched the glass. In that instant the parakeets became connected by some invisible thread. They swarmed to the opposite side of the cage. There they froze, motionless. Their fragile heads stared straight at us and their backs pressed against the far glass wall. Nestled together, they appeared to transform into one giant parakeet, too big for Nana's wire cage. Their beady black eyes didn't move from us. Never in my life had I seen birds so still, so watchful, so aware.

My mother arrived with the attendant, a young man with a beard and a concerned look. 'She just needs a replacement is all,' my mother was telling the attendant.

'Replacement?' The attendant's eyebrows pinched the bridge of his nose and he chewed his bottom lip.

My mom waved off the attendant's concern. 'We gave her first parakeet to her, um, neighbor.' My mom always wavered when she lied.

The attendant asked which one we wanted. My mother told Nana to pick.

'This is your *third* parakeet, right?' the man asked. A worrisome expression bled into his voice, which was as shaky as the parakeets.

'No,' Nana said. 'I'll only have this one.' She pointed to a gem-shaded parakeet with black spots on his belly.

The attendant stared at Nana, then at my mother. 'I picked out the other parakeets for you.' He said it as if he felt he needed to remind them.

'Yes. Third. That's right. She still has the other one,' my mother lied. The attendant also had to be protected from the truth. He retrieved the parakeet Nana wanted and placed him carefully in his travel box.

After he sealed the parakeet in the box, the attendant looked through the air holes with worried eyes. His shoulders sank as he handed the box to my mother. 'They don't have much meat on them. They're mostly bone and feather.'

'Who would eat that *flaquito*?' Nana shouted. She stomped her platform shoe against the floor. 'I'd rather go back to eating cats!'

My mother shoved Nana towards the exit. 'Thank you for the advice,' she said to the attendant. With one hand carrying the box and the other hand holding Nana's arm, my mother hurried out of the store. If I didn't follow, I would have been left behind.

We took Pepe III to his wire cage. He lived six weeks and then 'drowned'.

Before that happened, though, there was a day when my mother had to attend an overnight conference with my father and needed Nana to watch me and Titi. It was the first time I'd been there without my mother. Titi was outside by the pond, feeding the ducks crumbs of bread. I spent the first hour sitting on the couch, staring out the window at the traffic-congested street. The heat from all those cars made the world blurry, like gasoline in the air. I could *see* the humidity.

24

Nana asked if I wanted to hold Pepe III. Of the three Pepes, this one was the calmest, the most subordinate. He never pecked, never flapped his wings in an attempt to escape. Perhaps he had already accepted his fate. I began to think animals had access to truth in a way humans didn't. Animals don't need to be told anything. They just feel it.

While holding Pepe III, feeling his soft body made of toothpick bones and silk feathers, I said to Nana, 'Please don't hurt him.'

Nana gasped. She took up almost half of the couch. I feared I'd angered her. She could have easily drowned *me*. She held her hand to her chest and her brows went straight up past the curls of silver and black hair that hung down to her eyes. '*Dios mío*. I do not hurt my Pepes.'

The hyper but brittle patter of Pepe III's heart pounded into my thumb. I felt a pulsing connection between the two of us. I felt responsible for his life.

'What happened to the other Pepes?'

'Has your mother taught you Spanish yet?'

'No.'

'It makes better sense in Spanish, but I will try to tell you in English.' She went into the kitchen and opened the refrigerator. Alone with Pepe III, I opened my hands so that he could stand on my open palms, unrestricted by the chains of my fingers. If he wanted, he could have flown away. The sliding door leading to Nana's unscreened porch was open. The warm spring breeze teased the air of the apartment, beckoned the bird to soar. Instead, he balanced himself and stood there, facing me, obedient. Too obedient.

Nana returned with two glasses of orange juice, which she had hand squeezed that morning. She placed my glass on the wicker coffee table and sipped the juice from hers. Pulp stuck to her lips.

'In Cuba, I learned magic. Let me tell you about Yahubaba. Before Spaniards came to the island, there was a man who lived all by himself in a cave. His family had been taken by a hurricane, so he became very lonely and never left the cave. But inside the cave he could hear the voices of children coming from outside. He loved those voices, so one day he stepped outside and the sun was so bright it transformed him into a nightingale. He had a long, beautiful tail that was purple on the top and deep ocean blue on the bottom. His body was the color of dusk reflected in the sea. And he discovered that his voice sounded like children singing and playing. He spent the rest of his life flying above Cuba, singing the songs of youth and joy. That is what happened to the other Pepes. They are now nightingales soaring above Miami. I leave the back door and windows open so we can hear them. And maybe one day they will come back.'

'Is that a real story?' I asked.

'It's what my memory says.'

'You didn't make that up?'

Nana laughed so hard her dentures rattled and the couch shook. Her bracelets chimed against each other when she clapped her hands. 'One day,' she

26

said, 'you will tell your grandkids this story, and in that moment, your memory will create a new story.'

'Isn't that lying?'

Nana smiled and combed my hair with her fingers the way my mother did. I felt as fragile as the parakeet the instant she touched me.

'It is magic,' Nana said, her fingers drawing circles on my scalp, leaving trails of stardust in my imagination. 'Now drink your orange juice. The longer it sits, the more of its nutrients vanish.'

'Why didn't you just have Mom buy you a nightingale?'

'I told you. The story only makes sense in Spanish.'

'Can I watch you transform Pepe III into a nightingale?'

'Not yet,' Nana said. 'You're too young. But I can eventually teach you how to transform yourself into a nightingale, like Yahubaba. You'll have a long purple tail, too, and indigo wings that can fly you anywhere you want to go. And your voice! You'll be able to sing all the dreams that children have.'

Nana took Pepe III from me and held him close to her face. She made kissing noises with puckered lips. While staring at her parakeet, she said to me, 'You have to be careful, though. The wind will carry away *un flaquito* like you. You'll vanish.'

I sipped a mouthful of juice. Nana noticed me staring at her and rolled her eyes.

'*Mírate*,' she said. 'You don't have any meat. You're mostly bone and skin.'

My tongue drowned and all I could do was look at Pepe III, trying to imagine him as a much more majestic bird, eagle-sized, capable of withstanding the wind.

II

I hated the sight of briefcases waiting by the front door. At eleven, my age now qualified me to be left alone at home. I sat in the front room with my arms crossed as my father checked a folder, inserted it into the thinner briefcase, and went back to buttoning his shirt.

'Does my tie look okay?' he asked, pressing the wrinkles out of the olive-colored tongue hanging from his neck.

'I hate ties,' I said.

'What *don't* you hate?' my mother said and joined him, smiling in a way I'd never seen. They had secrets, which I also hated. The syrup smell of her perfume filled the room as my mother recited to me for the fifth time why I had to stay home alone. As a CPA, my father handled the financial operations for the municipality of Hialeah Gardens. He and my mother often went to dinner parties with the chief of police and the mayor. 'Not the type of people a child should be around,' she said. Her lips shined the red of a waxed apple. I remember standing by the front door, thinking I could guard it, prevent my parents from exiting into the world beyond our home. I stretched my arms, but my fingers barely touched the door frame. My mother interpreted my stance as a hug request. She bent down, squeezed me.

'Now move,' my father said.

'What happens if someone rings the doorbell?' I asked, still blocking the door.

'Don't answer it,' my father said.

'What if it's Titi?'

'She has a key.'

'What if a stranger takes her key and comes in?'

'Tell him to take his shoes off before stepping on the carpet,' my father said and finally moved me. His olive tie licked my head. 'You are almost twelve years old. Watch TV.'

When my parents left, all that remained were walls and floors, a vacuum of silence, as dense as the pressure at the bottom of the pool.

My father had recently bought a satellite dish for this very reason. Hundreds of channels provided me with a spectral reality that was supposed to exhaust my curiosity. With the TV, I could buy into the illusion that there was no absence. I had hundreds of channels, thousands of sequences that strung along a million shards of images a minute. Eventually the box would disappear and only the sights and sounds existed, whirring about the room like rollicking party guests. So when I made myself a bowl of cereal and spilled some milk on the burgundy throw rug, a pixelated woman, donning a clean white apron, appeared and pointed a static finger at me.

'Use Such-and-Such paper towels,' she said with maternal urging. 'They absorb twenty percent more liquid than the average brand.' The woman's static smile never changed. Her one-dimensional appearance made it easy to love her. All mothers should be so simple, I thought.

Other times, when I emptied my backpack onto the dining-room table, some cool kid from a show about high school appeared behind me and laughed at my half-hearted attempt to do homework. I heard the crisp and perfectly timed laugh track at the end of his jokes, despite them not being that funny. The air in his imagined presence had the sticky smell of hairspray. The other students, each of them appearing to be thirty-year-olds playing the part of high schoolers, high-fived him. They were right to mock me. I cared so little for school.

After a while, I could not tell whether my parents were home. The house with the TV on, so it was never silent, never seemed empty. It came to make no difference where my parents were. I began to associate their presence with the standard time slots of TV programming. 3–3.30pm: Late Lunch with Mom, starring Mom. 5.30–6pm: Home Alone Dos and Don'ts with Dad, starring Dad. Their eventual 6pm departures were as inevitable, and therefore emotionally expected, as the end of an episode. And if

Titi was home, which was rare, she became part of a hip, cool cast with a social import that demanded no more than thirty minutes (ninety if she was part of a movie special).

Titi, now seventeen, was nearing high school graduation and planned to go straight to work for Disney. Because she knew Disney didn't require good grades, she didn't take school seriously. Instead, when my parents left, so did she. Sometimes, though, she'd bring her glitter-splattered girlfriends with frizzy hair and bright outfits to the house. They would sit with me on the couch, rustle my hair, kiss my cheek. Sometimes they'd dance with me, swing me around, and bring me into my sister's bedroom. There, illuminated by her light-framed mirror, they'd discuss important plans for the evening. I tried memorizing what was said, but I didn't understand any of it. The tones of their voices signified that the dialogue would be instrumental later in the season. And then they'd leave me back on the couch, alone with the dazzling TV screen.

One night, after several hours alone, my parents came home in a season premier conflict. My father accused my mother of flirting with a deputy. She walked past me in such a flurry I thought she had come directly out of the TV. I tried recalling what show or movie she was from. Lost in the phantasmagoric haze into which my memory had been shaping, I leaned forward enough on the couch's edge to see down the hall into my parents' bedroom. My mother sat at her mahogany dressing table, unpinning her gold earrings and staring in the mirror. She liked what she saw, I could tell. Her smile turned her face dawn red. My father stood behind her and his face steamed a different color red.

'If you embarrass me like that again, we'll get a divorce,' he said. 'I promise you that.'

His suit looked too tight on him, ready to rip at the seams. I prayed and prayed that it wouldn't, that it would hold him inside.

'You are overreacting,' my mother said.

'You can take your son and get the hell out of here with *the deputy*. Live on his shitty salary. I'm tired of supporting a whore. There. Is *that* overreacting?'

'You can do better.'

A part of me felt drunk on what I witnessed. Of course, I didn't know at eleven what being drunk was like, but once I did I would always associate the feeling of drunkenness – destructive passion and an illogical outpour of emotions – with my parents' arguments. A much larger part of me felt overshadowed, forgotten in the fog of rage. Every audience member imagines himself the protagonist. Everyone wants to be on the other side of the screen, the center of the stage where personal problems become universal and everyone cares about your well-being. The dramatic conflict taking place between my parents seemed much more real than anything I'd ever seen, including *Cops* and all the other docudramas I watched at that age. This virtual immersion in reality excited me no end. But the truth remained: I was still a viewer, unimportant because the drama did not concern me.

I climbed down from the couch and stood in full view of my parents, telescoped by the hallway's parallel rows of picture frames. The bedroom light cast a glare on the glass of each picture. Faces glowed into obscurity. But not mine. The bedroom lamp was my stage light. There was no way my parents could *not* see me. I needed to be part of the cast.

Both of my parents noticed me, signaled by a collective sigh that fooled me into thinking they finally agreed, finally fused their purposes back into a singular one.

'Take your son,' one of them said.

'He's *your* son,' said the other.

*

What I realized later in my life is the sad condition of audiences everywhere. They are a burden to the actors, the writers, the producers, the directors, and the extras. Everything is done for their entertainment, but they are amorphous and without purpose. They have no identity. They don't matter. And all this only encourages their thirst for drama, because only the drama they consume can fill the void of an empty home with meaning. I was and always have been the prototypical voyeur, burdening those whom I watch with my deep interest in their lives, existing but not really existing. A personified object to be bartered. *If the walls could talk, their secrets would be worth millions.* And only I would buy them.

*

Finally, my mother's voice became distinguishable. 'He just wants attention.' She sounded firm and intelligent, confident she knew the problem of my standing in the hall for no apparent reason. 'We're never home because we have to appease your clients.'

My mother had the innocuously sarcastic quality of the *Golden Girls*. She sounded exactly like Dorothy Zbornak when she thanked President Bush for ignoring the nation's education issues.

'Call it what it is,' my father said, sneering at my mother. Already I was forgotten. 'Your favorite part is *appeasing* my clients.'

At some point, Titi returned home. She found me in the hallway and pulled me into my room. Her long blonde hair and fair skin were TV perfect. 'Go to bed,' she said.

'I want to watch.'

Titi guarded the door. Her presence seemed to mute my parents' voices. 'Trust me,' she said before closing my door. 'You are better off not watching any of it.'

*

My mother woke me the next morning and asked if I wanted to walk to the library. This was a walk I loved. Rows of palm trees lined the sidewalk, slashing shadows in the sunlight. I pretended I was trekking through a tropical jungle in search of some very important book. The sidewalk led to the bright green fields of the library's park. I'd cross the monkey bars, run up the slide, and swing on the tire tied to an oak – imagined obstacles guarding the treasured sacred texts. Inside the library, I'd spend hours collecting books on astrology, zoology, and ghosts. When my mother let me, I'd also check out anything written by Stephen King. In my mind, these books were left behind by ancient sages, intended to be read only by me.

On this day, though, I had trouble finding my reverie. The sun was too close to its zenith, out of the palm trees' reach. There was no breeze to cool the steaming air rising from the street's black pavement. A car accident had backed up traffic alongside the sidewalk, which spoiled the air with heavy fumes. The persistent chug of impatient engines clouded my ability to transform the world around me.

I walked next to my mother and wanted to hold her hand. Aware that eleven-year-olds don't hold their mothers' hands, I didn't. Instead, I stared at her sun-spotted fingers, dangling at her side. Stuck in the real world, I felt frightened. I considered asking if we could turn around, but when I opened my mouth to admit defeat, I instead asked, 'Why does Dad think you don't love him?'

My mother wore wide-rimmed sunglasses that shielded her entire face from the sun. They made her appear as though she could see for hundreds of miles. And at that moment her face was so serious, fixed so still out in front of us, that I thought maybe the glasses did enhance her vision. After a few seconds, she stopped walking and pulled me close to her.

'All this traffic is making it too hot,' she said. 'Let's go home. I'll take you to the library tomorrow.'

We turned around and walked at a much faster pace. My fear grew, rising in my throat. I wondered what deterred her: a car accident, a dangerous confrontation between two drivers, a wild tiger that escaped my imaginary jungle and was now loose on the streets? There was no telling what she saw. I did not have a pair of glasses like the ones she had.

By the time we reached the safety of our house, I had begun to wonder whether I had actually asked my original question. It would make sense that 'Can we go home?' and not 'Why does Dad think you don't love him?' would spur a sudden retreat. But I couldn't remember. My heart was still beating from running away from something.

I needed clarity. I found my mother fanning herself on the patio and asked her the question again.

'It's not even summer yet,' she said, staring into the pool with her glasses. They probably allowed her to see each hydrogen atom. 'Put on your bathing suit.'

Again, I felt uncertain as to what I had just asked. Somehow, I couldn't recall whether I'd said

37

something about the pool. As we stepped inside the house, I asked her once more. She hushed me and said, 'Let Dad sleep. He had a rough night.'

That was no answer. It was the basis for my question in the first place. As I became aware that my parents had secrets I would never know, I started understanding how alone I truly was. They had concerns beyond me, like appeasing deputies. I had no clue what that meant. Of course, I knew what flirting meant, but not what it meant for my mother to do it and for my father to be angry about it. And instead of clarity, my mother found ways to further confuse me. There was no reading my parents like they were books. Their pages didn't turn in any order.

*

A month later, my parents attended a municipal party in the Keys. Because they would be gone overnight, they left me with Nana while Titi stayed at a friend's house. Since my mother's refusal to buy Nana any more birds, Nana had softened. She stopped wearing shoulder pads and now appeared rounder. The loss of sharp angles provided her with a gentleness that invited compassion instead of fear. After a few hours of silently drawing while Nana played the organ, she asked me what I was hiding. Confused, I scanned my sketches of various superheroes, all invented by me, to see if I had left anything out. Once I realized she couldn't see my sketches and therefore could not be asking about them, I looked up at her. I felt parakeet-sized, helpless in her possession.

'If you aren't honest with yourself,' she said, 'you'll never transform into a nightingale. Deception is too heavy. Carry it and you'll never fly.' She turned on her seat so that her back faced the organ's keys, simple in their white and black pattern.

All I did was stare at her, twisting my pencil in my fingers.

She pressed down the chord of C major and then stood, the world shrinking underneath her. I expected a lecture, the speech that would enlighten me with an episode-ending epiphany.

'Let me make you a mamey shake,' she said.

She took two small mameys from the bowl in the living room. Both brown-skinned fruit fit in a single palm. I followed her into the kitchen, where she peeled each one and scooped the salmon-colored flesh into the blender. The shrill of the blade sent waves throughout the apartment.

'When my family first moved to Miami, I had to share a room with my sister. I was ten; she was fourteen. The room had two windows, one over each bed, and though we weren't in Cuba anymore, my mother insisted we cover each window with a mosquito net. It felt like the world had a mosquito net over it. The darkness between my sister's bed and mine went on forever. *Para siempre*. I had just fallen asleep when the smell of smoke woke me. I thought the house was on fire, but a silent one. A secret fire. It was like a whisper. *Como se dice un sueño* that startles you and keeps you awake because you heard it asleep and awake at the same time? Anyway, my sister was a quiet sleeper. She never snored.'

Nana poured milk into the blended mamey while she told her story.

'After a while, the blue haze molded the figure of a large man with broad shoulders. He stood in the dark part of the room and stared directly at me. *Que no tenía una cara*. His eyes gone. The two sockets were dark like the room. He had badges on his sash, epaulettes, a campaign hat tucked under his arm. He was *un soldado por Batista*. The loneliness of this man terrified me. I was always alone as a child.'

Nana stopped the blender and stared up at the ceiling, as if she could see through it. She had her back to me, but I imagined her face tense, holding back tears.

'My mother took my sister shopping all the time and left me at home. My sister was her favorite. I was supposed to be an abortion, but she found out about me too late. *Ay*, I'd never felt loneliness like this *soldado*. I jumped into bed with my sister, as I always did when I had a nightmare, but my sister was gone.'

She then lowered her eyes to me, and in them was the same heaviness my mother had in her eyes while telling my father years later about the dementia running through the family.

'I screamed. *El soldado* stood there, a terrifying emptiness where eyes should have been. He remained still and depressed. I screamed until my voice cracked. When I couldn't take looking at this man anymore, I lunged for the door and darted down the hall, flipping on every light. Every room was empty. My aunt, gone. My parents, gone. Even our poodle, Napoleon, gone. I sat against the wall in the kitchen, tucking my knees to my forehead so I couldn't see the blue haze spreading like smoke throughout the house. The haze had no smell. I expected fire, but the smoke was nothing.'

She stopped talking, stopped blending the shake. The brown skin of the fruit sat on the counter like it had been there for years. The world stood still.

'The loud knocks at the front door could not get me to move. I had given up, had realized that my family abandoned me to the ghosts of this house, *la historia de nuestra isla abandonado*. Let what may come. The haze stretched for my feet, and as it approached I felt the cold of the ghost. My toes went numb. I sat there drumming my forehead against my knees and crying, unable to bear the feeling.

'Finally, the loud knocks turned into the sound of a key unlocking the door. Someone came running into the kitchen and I saw that it was our neighbor. He scooped me up and held me. I was a little girl then that could fit over someone's forearm.

'"Dunadlfkuyfklds?" he said and stroked my hair. "Alkusdklfnlkd?"

'I hated America. I hated the English that people spoke. *Ay*, I missed Cuba. I cried into this strange man's shoulder. The haze had already reached me, had already filled me with the ghost's eyeless stare. That feeling would forever haunt my memory.

'"Klafudka fhidkfudikflu dudkhjf," the neighbor said. "Alku dkdhjhjeue? Jdudneh qppiew cndu?"'

Nana turned to me. Her face was as red as the mamey pulp. She waved her hands while imitating the neighbor's garbled English.

'The only reason I knew he wasn't a ghost was because I could feel his warmth, his goodness, his *cigarro* breath. I begged him to find my family, but I begged him in Spanish, a language he did not know. Though I knew he was good, I no longer felt safe in his arms. We couldn't speak. He couldn't help me.

'I pushed out of his arms and stood on my own. No matter how much I wiped away my tears, more kept coming.

'"Where's my mom?" I asked, but he didn't know what *dónde mi mama* meant. He stared at me stupidly, his big, round blue eyes glazed over, looking like a fish.

'Not until my family returned home a few hours later would I find out they had gone to a reception at my sister's dance studio. They left the next-door neighbor, Steven, a man who they knew could not speak to me, in charge of watching me. *Ay*.' She sighed, and then continued. 'Once things settled down, I begged my father to let me sleep in bed with him and my mother. He stomped his feet on the ground, which he did to scare his children into silence. But I kept begging. Finally, he threatened to slap me if I didn't go back to my room. If it weren't for my sister, *Dios mío*, I don't know what I would have done going back to that room alone. Before I could finish crying, my father then scolded me for turning on every light and wasting the electricity.'

Nana handed me a glass of gooey red mamey.

'When Mom and Dad fight,' I said, 'I feel like the ghost.'

'*Pobrecito*.' She pet my head, as she always did when sympathizing with me.

'My heart beats faster the louder Dad yells. My head echoes with his anger. Then Mom screams at him. Then I turn invisible.'

Nana shook her head in that disappointed way that let me know she was on my side. Then she taught me my first magic trick.

The plan was hers. A couple hours before my parents were expected to return, Nana dropped me off at my house. I chose the largest butcher knife I could find in the kitchen and basted it with ketchup. Then, I sliced a tear in my t-shirt from my collar to the waist, reapplying ketchup as needed. Not knowing what a suicide was supposed to look like, I stabbed everywhere, jabbing the knife into my stomach, slashing my thighs and arms. I sliced off my ear, then thought that was probably going too far so reattached it. I X-ed out my face, mistakenly

43

making the cuts too straight, too deliberate. The steel blade of the knife sent cold shivers into my flesh. My body trembled from its touch. I imagined the knife not cutting, but sewing me together, as if I'd crumble into shards of glass without deeper seams. My pain was a paradox. It always has been. To my chagrin, my appearance began to resemble a sort of spoof on Stephen King's *Carrie*. I was too young to understand subtlety. My body became a pincushion, taking the wanton and gratuitous stabs. When I could no longer stand, I sprawled on the floor, swallowing the ketchup that dripped from my nose and ears, all too perfect wounds.

By the time my parents arrived, they found me in a tomato-sauce massacre in the center of the beige-carpeted living room.

'Real nice,' my father said, not a smidgen of horror in his voice. 'Look what *your* son did to the carpet.'

I kept my eyes closed, hoping beyond hope that he would notice me differently. Walk in a second time. See that his son had committed suicide at a startlingly young age. Blame himself, blame my mother. Take notice. 'I am also insecure,' my illusion was trying to say.

'Go wash up and get in bed,' my mother ordered.

'This is the kind of babysitting your mother does?' my father said. It seemed like he purposely avoided looking at me. 'This isn't any better than how those birds turned out.'

My mother pulled me to my feet and held my face. With my chin in her hand, it felt like floating, like she'd lifted me from the ground. She looked tired, her heavy eyes barely capable of remaining open. 'We'll go see a movie in the morning.' Her expectant, unsurprised voice sounded as though I simply had mud on my feet. Still, I accepted the bargain and went to the shower.

When Nana heard of the less-than-successful outcome of my first attempt at illusion, she laughed and said I had forgotten the most important ingredient.

What was that ingredient?

'Worcestershire sauce,' she said, her dentures rattling in her delight, 'to darken the unnaturally bright ketchup.'

III

According to Nana, illusion served three potential purposes:
1. Help others see their condition more clearly.
2. Help yourself see your condition more clearly.
3. Cloud or confuse others, or your own ability to see at all.

The third purpose, Nana said, was to be avoided at all costs. Deception should always lead to truth, she reminded me over and over again. 'Besides,' Nana also said, 'all someone has to do to keep himself from seeing is drink rum.'

Becoming *un gran ilusionista*, as Nana called it, was a lot more difficult than understanding those three steps. Despite her ostensible allegiance to Catholicism, she often told me the story of Adechina Remigio Herrera, the legendary babalawo, or sacred priest, responsible for introducing Regla de Ocha to Cuba. Brought to the island as a slave, Adechina disguised the deities he worshipped in Africa by referring to them with Catholic names. Sakpata became San Lázaro. Shango became Santa Barbara. But not really. The deities didn't lose themselves in their disguises. They became more recognizable, able to survive violent persecution from the enslavers. The illusion that Santería was the same as Catholicism led to Adechina's eventual freedom and prosperity as a landowner.

'Imagine,' Nana would say, 'how easy it would have been for him to lose himself in his own illusion, confusing saints with orishas. Instead, his vision remained clear.' The one thing Nana always warned me about was that if an artist forgot the purpose of the illusion being cast, the illusion took over, became the master. The person, who thought he was the conductor, became the trick, the artifice, something cast and diffused like cigarette ash the moment the audience lost interest. 'Do not let your illusion take over,' she warned.

Then she pulled a container of ice cream out of her closet and scooped warm, melted slush into a bowl.

*

About twice a week, I would raise my hand in my sixth-grade math class, tell the teacher I was going to throw up, stick my finger down my throat, and actually throw up. The administrator would call to have someone pick me up. Of course, my parents were both at work, so they'd call Nana. Each time Nana came to get me, the principal suggested I see a gastrologist.

'His teacher says uncontrollable flatulence disrupts the other classmates,' the principal said, sounding more irritated than concerned. 'They tease Tito by calling him "Skunkface".'

'Skunkface,' Nana repeated, as if learning the word. Nana played the part of supporting character perfectly, each time sounding shocked.

The principal nodded. Her gold hair waved down onto her shrugging shoulders. Her frown signaled her clear discomfort with the conversation.

'Is it okay to bully kids at this school?'

The principal's eyes shot open, as if someone had just dumped ice into her blazer. 'Of course not. I'm sorry. That isn't—'

'Do all the kids have embarrassing nicknames?'

I summoned a burp from deep inside my stomach's gaseous pit, exhaling from my nostrils to send the stench towards the principal.

'Those kids will be dealt with, I assure you.' The principal stood and walked us to the door.

(For the record, those kids were never 'dealt with'.)

After promising the principal that I would be on a bland diet for the remainder of the day, Nana drove me to Burger King. We placed our order over the intercom, but Nana's thick accent and discomfort with English in general made communicating the best entertainment. I knew which words that, when she said them, sounded like curses. For instance, she pronounced both 'fog' and 'fork' as 'fuck'.

At the end of the order, I told Nana to insist that we got a fork and napkin.

In my memory, the words came out as clear as a chlorinated pool: 'Give me a fucking napkin.'

'Excuse me?' the lady said over the intercom.

'My grandson wants a fucking napkin.'

All the while I laughed uncontrollably. The confused, offended look on the teller handing us our food amused me to no end.

When we drove away, Nana looked at me with a knowing grin and winked.

'You naughty boy, Tito-my-love,' she said using a tone of such irony even I, a child, detected it. 'Taking advantage of an old lady.'

From there, we went to the movies. In the darkness of the theater, I could speak more openly to Nana. I whispered to her that I held on to my father's feet when he left for work in the morning. I whispered that I screamed in the middle of the night for no reason so that my mother would sleep in my bed. I looked forward to her quiet entrance, tiptoeing to my room. I loved the way she smelled of copy paper. I needed their presence – the sound of my father's heavy feet dragging against tile, the melody of my mother's words when she wished me goodnight. I whispered to Nana that my father insisted I was too old to have my mother sleep in bed with me.

'Loneliness is a terrible thing,' she said as a T-Rex chased a Jeep on the movie screen. Despite the intense music and the ancient beast's hungry roars, Nana's voice sounded clear and assuring.

'*Locura tiene más compañeros y asistentes que el sentido común hace,*' she said, quoting Don Quixote. I was not able to translate this until I learned her language. At the time, rather than wisdom, her advice sounded like music.

*

Often, while visiting Nana's apartment, I'd browse her complete collection of the *Encyclopaedia Britannica*. Their hard navy covers with gold trim felt heavy with possibility, as if each glossy page presented a dimension I could enter – a country to visit, an animal to morph into, a time period to live in. Impressed by the movie we had just seen, I was looking up 'Velociraptor' when I came upon a folded piece of paper with the word 'Vanity' written on it.

Something about how fragile the paper felt – brittle enough to crumble between my fingers – made me feel as though I shouldn't open it. I looked up from the couch, but Nana was distracted with the laundry, which she was washing in her bathtub. She said she needed my mother to show her how to use the washing machine she'd had for the past eight years.

I peeled the note open. The paper could have been torn from a journal. It had a rich texture that stood the test of time, though it was yellowing and curling at the edges. The actual note was written in a swift cursive, in black ink that hadn't faded, but

I instantly recognized the Spanish. The note was signed by Manny, my grandfather.

I never met my grandfather. He had left Nana and returned to Cuba once and for all. What I knew of him, I heard from my mother. She told me how he went to the University of Havana to become an accountant, but instead became an anthropologist. He studied indigenous Cuban culture. Later, he taught at the university. My mother said his favorite story to tell was about a man named Yahubaba who transformed into a nightingale. After the revolution, though, the government began investigating him. 'Nana thought it was too dangerous to keep going back,' I remember my mother telling me. 'Then something in Dada broke. He stopped telling stories.'

Nana never talked about Manny. I worried that showing her the note would anger her. Somehow, I had to decipher it on my own.

Hoping to glean some kind of clue, I read the encyclopedia entry on Vanity, but couldn't connect any of the ideas with the note. Did Manny commit a deadly sin? Should I look for an oval mirror hanging in a bathroom? Did Manny think too highly of himself? Did Nana think too highly of herself? I wondered how highly I thought of *my*self.

I memorized the individual words in Spanish and, on different days and out of sequence, asked Nana what each one meant.

After almost a month, I had it somewhat translated: *Sorry I don't make you happy. Invisible, I am more.*

Nana always swore that illusion was empathy (and never the other way around). If one could feel the way others felt, they could influence those feelings – the foundation of magic. But one had to be sensitive, had to feel the tears streak down others' faces, had to recognize the brightness of ketchup, had to memorize the rehearsed words of prayers. Illusionists, she explained, moved people not by force but by willing others to move themselves.

Invisible, I am more.

I thought about those words, saying them again and again in my mind. I dreamed about becoming invisible. That phrase became a chant – the code to the illusion I'd become.

*

At first I used my mother's eyeshadow to paint a black and blue bruise under my eye. Teachers at school doted on me, brushing my hair back away from my forehead while whispering small prayers. I kept my head down to hide the imprudent application of make-up, but my teachers must have interpreted this as a show of shame. They asked a series of questions, the answers to which could have been used to prosecute someone in court.

'Is there anything you want to talk about?'

'Did you get into a fight?'

'Did someone in your family do this?'

'Are you too scared to speak?'

My failure to prepare a story worked to my advantage as my teachers interpreted my silence as a trauma that needed constant nurturing. My math and science teacher insisted I eat with her at lunch, during which she shared her yogurt and banana and later bought me a fresh-baked cookie from the cafeteria. While we ate, she'd reach over and rub my back, and so much of me wanted to sidle closer to her so her arm went all the way round my shoulders. So I'd feel held.

The other students' reactions ranged from admiration to provocation. Some wanted to stare at my black eye in awe. Some wanted to touch it, but I insisted the pain was too great and fortunately they respected my apparent intolerance. The only snafu was with Bloody-Nose-Christian, who got his name after he broke the noses on three different kids in a single week. He walked up to me during recess and punched me in the stomach. The air wheezed out of my lungs and I hunched over, collapsed on the dry, sharp grass. 'Not so tough,' he said and walked away.

At least he spared my nose.

Despite that one incident, the trick was overall a success, until the principal called home and started asking my mom personal questions. She came into my room when I was kicking around my action figures. She gripped my chin tight in her hand.

'What black eye?' she asked.

Nana had washed it off before Mom got home. I gave her a look of confusion, as if she had asked me a question in another language.

Later, she told my father and I heard them through the wall dividing my room from theirs.

'He's so silent,' my mom said. 'He keeps to himself.'

'You know who he reminds me of?' my dad asked, rhetorically because he already knew who. 'Your mother. He's all secrets.'

'Maybe I should stay home with him. I could take calls from home.'

'If you start taking calls from home, there's no reason we'd have to stay in Miami.'

My father badly wanted to move. He believed everyone in Miami had formed a cabal to plot against him. *Everyone.* He still blamed my mother for flirting with deputies and other uniformed men. He fired the cleaning crew at his office because he thought they were stealing general ledgers. He once claimed the mayor wanted to have him killed because he wouldn't falsify tax documents. (My father held onto numbers and tax laws like they were all that existed.) In reality, his paranoia had little to do with Miami. Even years after we would finally move, he would insist on sitting with his back to the wall whenever we went out to eat, keeping everyone in sight.

But I suspected a more insidious reason for wanting to move. He wanted to be farther away from Nana. On several occasions he complained that 'she's always here. And even when she's not physically here, I can still sense her presence.'

At his suggestion to move I stopped listening, kicked Spiderman, and jumped into bed. I did not want to leave. At the same time, I couldn't deny the hope in my heart at my mother's suggestion of taking calls from home, of being home.

A week later, my mother said she'd leave work early to pick me up from school. From there, she promised, we'd go to the comic book store, get ice cream, and spend the rest of the day swimming in our pool, in which we hadn't swum in almost a year. While waiting in the courtyard after school for her van to enter the pick-up loop, I chewed my lips. My teeth gnashed the thin layer of skin as if it was a strip of Delmonico steak. Already I could taste puddles of iron, metallic, like a bad day at the dentist, but I kept masticating, building up reserves. I didn't swallow or spit. By the time I noticed the pearl white of her van, I was ready to drown.

As I climbed in the passenger seat, my mom asked what I wanted first – ice cream or comics. I looked at her with my eyes swollen and wet from the sour taste in my mouth. Already, her face, powdered and calm and pretty from her short day at the office, darkened. Before I could read her emotion – confusion or horror, shock or disappointment? – I parted my lips just a sliver and let blood drip down my chin and onto my yellow and green school uniform and her beige cloth seat.

'My God!' my mother screamed.

But her outburst sounded as though it were charged by an equal amount of concern and annoyance. I couldn't lose her, not now. This was my stage and it was up to me to affect authenticity, to draw sympathy from the audience. I remembered Nana's advice: the audience *must* believe that the performer is in danger. No risk, no magic. Love, I believed, was an emotion that could be willed, not by the person who felt love, but by the person who wanted to feel loved. This belief was the greatest gift Nana left me. This was, I thought, the meaning of vanity.

I blinked the water building behind my eyes and incorporated the fortuitous effect into my act. I coughed and sobbed and stained everything. The blood dripped down to my socks.

'What in God's name is going on with you?' my mom asked as she pulled into a parking space.

'He hit me,' I said, although purely by instinct. I did not have a planned explanation to develop this statement.

'Who hit you?'

'Bloody-Nose-Christian.'

'Who?'

'He said I had too much vanity.' And to save myself I mumbled incoherently and forced heavier sobs.

However, I would have been better off giving her a story, any story. My mother, furious now, turned off the car, walked around to my side of it, and pulled me to her side. She dragged me back towards the school, me riding the hot waves of her wake.

I knew I was in trouble now, but I couldn't help feeling ecstatic at my mother's mad, passionate fury, fueled by deep love.

Of course, the principal hadn't heard of any altercation. She filed a report and suggested that my mother look into a doctor, one who helps children who 'self-mutilate'.

At the principal's suggestion, my mother exploded. 'My son is not some druggie suicidal maniac,' she said. 'What do you mean, "self-mutilate"? He is loved at home.'

She threatened to pull me out of the school and then stormed out of the principal's office. No matter how much I begged her not to, she told my father. Through the wall I heard him say he'd found a house in Orlando. 'You'll be four hours from your mother,' he said. 'Tito can go to school with normal kids who don't self-mutilate.'

'No. The principal thinks *he's* the one who self-mutilates.'

'The principal?' My father laughed, as if he'd finally caught one of his conspirators. 'I don't trust that woman at all.'

My mother cried.

IV

The taste of solid paste filled my mouth. It was heavy, like wet cement dripping down my esophagus. Every time I imagined the Barium, deceptively creamy and white like dessert, I wanted to vomit – but that was what got me here in the first place.

The walls in the X-ray room shone the same color white. I hadn't eaten in twenty-four hours and the flat lighting made me dizzy. It felt like my neck no longer existed, as though only the fluoroscope connected my head, keeping it from floating up to the ceiling. As the radiologist explained how images of my stomach would be recorded, I closed my eyes and repeated Manny's phrase to myself: Invisible, I am more.

A few weeks later, my mother and I returned to the doctor who had ordered the X-ray. He said the results of the upper-GI were good – no ulcers. However, he also believed I was a candidate for gastritis. 'His stomach lining looks very thin,' he said. 'If he's *dumping* most of the food he eats, the acids will burn right through his digestive system.'

The doctor's fat cheeks pinched his quarter-sized glasses as he read notes from the pink pages of his file. My mother stared at me, her hand over her mouth, as if I had gotten myself into the worst possible trouble. I felt indicted by her stare. There wasn't much compassion, only a knowing impatience.

Later, when my father heard the diagnosis, he also indicted me with his stare. During dinner, under the flat kitchen lights, I could feel both of them watching me, counting how many bites I took of my steak and green beans. It was like they willed each forkful into my mouth. I had no control over my hand, no say in the performance commanded by their gaze.

'It could just be nerves,' my father said through a mouthful of food. 'Dealing with a bully can be tough.'

Titi stood up from the table and brought her plate to the sink. She rinsed it, placed it on the drying rack, and then grabbed her keys.

'We haven't finished,' my father said.

'I'm sorry,' Titi hissed. 'I'm going to a movie that starts in thirty minutes. I prefer my fiction projected on a screen.' Before she headed for the front door, she shot me a look that I did not quite get. What did she know that I didn't?

'One teacher caught him forcing himself to throw up,' my mother reminded him. Both of their tones sounded rehearsed, like actors on made-for-TV comedies.

My father chewed and swallowed. He stared at me until I did the same. Two green beans down. Three total. Six ounces of steak and fourteen more green beans left.

'Stay home with him,' my father said. 'He needs you.'

'I need to go to Nana's,' I said. 'She'll know what to do.'

My father laughed in that sarcastic way he did when he heard bad news. Then his face became serious as he glanced at my mother. His steel-colored eyes narrowed, sharp, like a two-tined fork. I could tell my mother felt them because she winced.

She rubbed my father's back and looked at me, mimicking my father's sharp stare. 'Get started on your nutrition shakes and prove that you don't need me to watch you,' she said.

Following the doctor's recommendation, I was told to drink Ensure after each meal. The supposed 'milkshakes' tasted no different than the Barium. When it came time to drink each bottle, my mother watched me with a stern impatience.

'I'd rather have a mamey shake,' I said.

But my preference didn't matter. I had to show her an empty bottle and mouth before I could be free of her watch. She had grown wise to magic.

*

A day or so later, Titi burst through the front door holding a mud-colored cocker spaniel, its fur matted with blood.

'Two kids were throwing rocks at this poor thing behind the 7-Eleven,' she said. The dog's face looked like someone had kicked it.

61

My mother calmed my sister while petting the trembling animal. Spots on its body had turned black from the dried blood. My mother didn't seem to mind and took the tangled mess from my sister. She told me to stay home while she and Titi went to the vet. Naively, I'd hoped they would leave it there. While I had always wanted a pet, there was no more room for tragedy in this house. Bloody-Nose-Christian punching me in the stomach didn't compare to whatever this dog had experienced.

When they returned a few hours later, Titi still had the spaniel pressed against her chest. The dog had been shaved. Its pale body had bruises and stitches all over it. It appeared to be smiling, its tongue dripping stupidly. It had all the love and affection in the world in that moment. All it had to do was be abused almost to the point of death. Nana was right. The presence of danger guarantees notice.

Titi brought the dog to me and said, '*I* saved Ginger's life.'

She held up her nose, as if she had become some hero to be worshipped.

'We're keeping it?' I asked, looking at my mother in desperation.

Titi looked at me as though I were a monster, as though I terrified her. She sat on the couch with Ginger on her lap and talked in that high-pitched condescending way adults talk to babies: 'Aren't you so precious? Yes you are. No one will ever forget your precious face.'

V

While I still wasn't allowed to go to Nana's, Nana could come over to the house. She and I sat out by the pool, with our feet dangling in the water. Nana was telling me that all I needed was Cuban food: *platanitos*, *ropa viejo*, *picadillo*, *frijoles negros*. 'Those shakes are nothing but air,' she complained. The end of her blue skirt floated in the pool. The material became the same color, making it seem like Nana extended from the water.

'I did this to myself,' I said, quietly so no one else could hear. My father was at the office and my mother was working inside the house. Still, I couldn't be sure only Nana could hear me. I was scared – of my stomach pains, of the fact I had lost ten pounds in a month, of the way my mother cried one night while telling my sister I could develop stomach cancer.

'How do I stop it?' I kicked pool water up into the air. Just telling Nana made me want to hunch over. My gut was in a knot.

'How?' She tilted her head down so that she could look at me over the top of her auburn sunglasses. To let me know she was worried, not angry, she combed my hair away from my forehead. The sunlight spilled over her and cast a glare on the pool water.

I took Manny's note out of my pocket and handed it to her. At first, she stared at it without moving, as if the note cast a freezing spell on her. In the silence of her stillness, I became afraid I had done something very wrong. Everything was upside down. I was supposed to be casting an illusion that would make everyone – anyone – love me. Instead, it seemed I did nothing but cause pain to everyone. This was how I tried winning love: by hurting those I wanted to love me. Finally, Nana moved, but it was only a couple of blinks that flicked tears onto her already soaked blue skirt. A second later, she became a fountain.

'The only certain way to exist is to be remembered,' she said. 'Or is it to be the remember*er*? I forget which.'

'I want someone to remember me.'

'In Cuba there was an old woman with a lot of money who owned land near Canal de Entrada. She could see both La Cabaña and Morro Castle. She had the view to herself. Her husband was *un capitan* under Machado. He would catch her in bed with other men, but he could do nothing because of *el estado*. Imagine word getting out that a military man couldn't control his wife.' She laughed.

'As soon as Batista took over, he left her. Every morning the old woman put up posters of him. By night, the posters had been taken down. When she asked about his whereabouts, people pushed past her. No one spoke to her. Most people didn't bother noticing her at all. Her husband was never heard from again. Not even his name remained. *Sin nombre.*'

Nana started speaking faster, like her story was a song.

'Her children and grandchildren moved far away. Her family blamed her for her husband's disappearance. But they did send flowers on their wedding anniversary. No matter what, *Cubanos no se olvide su madres*. The old woman once brought all the flowers and all the unsigned cards to her husband's mother's house. "Please don't leave me alone," she cried, but no one came to the door. She opened her arms to heaven and let the petals fall. *Imagínate*, flowers piling at her feet. It was like she became a memory shared by no one.

'In her old age, her own memory started to deteriorate, and whenever she forgot something, it disappeared in real life. She forgot all the money she owned, so she became poor. She forgot her white *hacienda* with gardens of all kinds of flowers, so she slept under a tree. She forgot all the servants she had, so they became free. When she forgot a son or a daughter, it was like that person was never born. Her favorite daughter, *la más bella*, had moved to Puerto Rico. The moment the old woman forgot her was when the daughter was diving off a cliff into the sea. Her husband had been swimming in the water, watching his wife jump. When she disappeared, he stared at the sky for a long time before he started crying. The old woman's in-laws vanished while walking along the Malecón. People nearby saw a wave crash against the giant cement wall of the Malecón. The spray of water exploded in the air and fell like millions of diamonds onto the street. The mist cleared, and so did the in-laws. People searched the rocks at the bottom of the Malecón and found a dress and boater hat. Everyone assumed they had jumped. People whom the old woman had met on the street while looking for her husband disappeared. They couldn't remember her but she remembered them, up until they disappeared, that is.'

Birds flew overhead. Nana paused to watch, as if entranced by them. Once they disappeared into the woods behind the house, she continued.

'Word got out of the power this woman's sorrow had. Soon, everyone related to her ran back to her side. Her family became worried that they, too, would vanish. Relatives and people pretending to be relatives begged her forgiveness, kissed her papier-mâché hands, and performed *misas* for her day and night. They tried thinking of ways to make themselves more memorable. One man arrived at her house in a hot air balloon. Others arrived in large groups with ornate sets of china as gifts. Teachers led schools of children in ties and jackets, singing patriotic songs. *Pero*, they were all too late. One by one their skin became light and their eyes went hollow. *Entonces*, the breeze from the sea passed and carried them away.'

'How did she do it?' I asked.

'When she ran out of happy memories, she forgot how to be happy. And when she ran out of funny memories, she forgot how to laugh. It wasn't long before everything that gave her pain vanished for good. And when that time came, when the old woman had nothing left of herself to remember, she, too, disappeared. The kids in Havana told stories of her home. If you went inside, you could find her white nightgown with the rows of silver beads stitched along the waist in a puddle by the window. I don't know if that's true. I don't know anyone who went inside.'

'But you remember her,' I said.

'*¿Y qué?* Is it enough to be remembered? Or do you have to be the one remembering?'

'I don't understand.'

Nana looked around the backyard, as if she expected to find the old woman hiding behind a palm tree.

I stared at the note folded in Nana's hands and felt compelled to retrieve it. It belonged to her, I knew, but so much of my existence seemed to depend on it. I didn't know much about Manny or Cuba, but he had willingly disappeared and left behind clues. There had to be something related to the note that could help me. The air outside felt hot and still, as if God was holding his breath.

'It takes *un gran ilusionista* to reverse an illusion,' she said.

'But you're *una gran ilusionista*.'

'My memory is leaving me. Soon I will forget myself.' Nana pushed her sunglasses closer to her face, sealing her vision, and looked up at the sky. She took a deep breath, filling her chest with the hot air, as she folded the letter into a tiny square and slid it into her bra. I could hear the paper crinkle as her chest continued to expand.

I wanted to apologize, but somehow sensed that Nana wanted to do the same.

*

Nana and I dried off our feet, but the pool water still dripped from her blue skirt. Though we were now under the shade of the porch, Nana kept her sunglasses on. Tears stained her cheeks. She held my shoulders and told me, 'If we don't reverse the illusion, the wind will carry you away.'

I shivered in the cool of the shade, despite the fact the early summer heat already felt like August. 'What is vanity?'

Nana smiled at my question. She wrung the water from her skirt and used her wet hands to wipe the tear stains from her face. 'Vanity Bay Marina,' she said. 'Manny's best friend owned it. He probably arranged for Manny to leave from the marina.'

'Can we go see it? Maybe he left some clue.'

Nana held her hand over her chest, where the note was. 'He left his only clue.'

'What if you don't remember how to reverse a spell?' My voice grew louder. 'What if I disappear forever?'

Nana hushed me. She pulled me into a hug, rocking her body back and forth. It felt like riding the wind, comforting with cosmic grace. Instead, I knew vanishing would feel nothing of the sort. I imagined a hurricane tearing me apart.

'I wish I hadn't bullied him so much,' she said. 'I told him Cuba would never be our home, especially when his family had just been arrested by the police. And yet I called *him* the coward.'

'Maybe we can reverse both our illusions,' I said.

A gust of wind blew through the porch, almost ripping my towel from around my shoulders. Ginger barked from inside the house. Nana's skirt whipped around her like the wings of a swan and when it settled, she had the look of someone lost in deep thought, of someone who had to sort through millions of memories to find the one that mattered.

*

Nana parked her car in front of a blue warehouse that looked ten stories tall. A manatee was painted on a sign that read, Vanity Bay Marina. We walked along a boardwalk leading to several piers, all of them wide enough to tightrope walk. The sun bounced off all the white sailboats, skiffs, fishing boats, and canvas toppers. The reflective fiberglass created glares that pierced through my sunglasses.

'How did Manny get to Cuba?' I imagined him sailing on a one-person boat, arriving to Cuba like a lone adventurer the way my school depicted Christopher Columbus's arrival.

'I don't know,' Nana said. 'I've never been here.' For the first time in my life, I heard uncertainty and fear in Nana's voice.

Rows of boats set in giant iron hangars filled the warehouse. While standing there, I watched as a crane lifted a single-engine catamaran from the fifth row and slowly lowered it. Its double hulls looked like cannons ready to fire. When the crane moved the catamaran to the pier, Nana pulled me to her side. We were on our way to the shack leaning against the warehouse's blue wall.

Everything inside the shack smelled like seaweed. The only person in the store, a man with cotton hair and leathery skin, counted money on the counter. He had fishhooks and neon-colored worms, which looked like candy, scattered in front of him.

'¿*Lo conoces Mañuel?*' Nana asked.

'¿*Quien?*' He didn't stop counting the money. The stack of green paper seemed to be endless. In his obvious distraction, I considered snatching one of those gummy worms.

Nana explained that Manny was friends with Oro, the owner of the marina. The man finished counting and set the money in the register. Then, noticing me reach for a red and yellow worm, scooped the supplies on the counter and tossed them on a shelf behind him. He seemed angry at the two of us. The muscles on his shoulders tensed like electric shocks ran through his body. He shifted his weight from side to side, as if ready for a boxing match. When he told Nana something in Spanish, spit flew onto the counter.

Nana looked at me, lifted her sunglasses, and showed me the disappointment in her eyes.

Then, in English, the man said to me, 'I wouldn't let anyone leave for Cuba from my shop. I'll have nothing to do with that Communist dump.'

Back in the car, which had become an oven in the heat, Nana cried again.

'In America, as an immigrant, we had to be invisible,' Nana said. 'But Manny couldn't stand being invisible. *Ay, lo triste de verlo.* To see how much weight he lost, how his skin turned gray. It broke my heart. He was disappearing.' She swallowed and held a hand over her heart. This was the first time Nana spoke to me about Manny. 'Once you leave your home, you keep going. *Si no lo haces,* you forget who you are. He returned to Cuba to help his cousins, who had become political prisoners, and I never heard from him again. *Entonces*, he became invisible one way or the other.'

I felt guilty for her tears, as if I were the one who made Manny disappear.

71

'All I had were these little notes he left behind for me. Every few months I'd find a new one, like he was still around writing them.'

I leaned over and hugged her, not caring how the sweat made our skin stick. She smelled like over-cooked bread, burnt crust and all, but I didn't mind that either. Soon, my nose would be invisible, and I didn't know whether invisible noses could smell.

*

When Nana and I returned from Vanity Bay Marina, we were greeted by laughter. This came as a surprise, as both Nana and I were certain we'd get in trouble for breaking my father's visitation guidelines by leaving the house. Holding an unlit cigarette between his fingers, my father hugged Nana and then me. He introduced us to a man in a black suit with hair like a chestnut-colored puff.

'This is Carlos,' my father said, smiling like I'd never seen him smile before. 'He is going to sell this haunted house of ours.'

Carlos laughed the way one laughs when nothing funny happened. He had the genuine quality of a game show host.

'Where will we live?' I asked.

My mother cast a glance that hit me like a whip. It stung me into silence, but it came too late. My father had already heard the question and intended to answer it.

'We're moving to Orlando.'

When he said this, Nana held my hand.

Titi was in her room, already deciding what she would take with her. She tossed old clothes and spiral notebooks into a trash bag. It was so easy for her to dispose of unwanted memories.

'I'll visit my clients in Miami once a month. The rest of the time, Penny can raise Tito in a reasonable city – one without high crime rates and stress. We'll be fifteen minutes from Disney, where Titi has always wanted to work!' He lit his cigarette inside the house. The smoke rose and gathered at the ceiling, hovering above like a curious ghost.

'When you play a sport in Orlando,' my father said to me, smoke pouring from his mouth, 'you don't have to go up against thousands of kids, like you would in this crowded city.'

He offered Carlos a cigarette, but he refused. Instead, Carlos collected some papers and slid them into a black briefcase. As he and my father headed to the front door, Carlos told me not to try out for football. 'You're too small,' he said. 'You'd be the football.'

'I don't like sports,' I said.

My father held the door open for Carlos and then followed him outside. With them gone, my mother clasped her hands and looked at Nana. It was the gesture she made when she prayed. 'I'm sorry,' she said.

Titi ran to my father and hugged him. They celebrated like they'd just won the lottery.

The smoke-ghost lingered. It made the air smell rancid. Nana waved her hand in front of her and knelt. She kissed me on the forehead. Before I realized what was going on, Nana was gone.

VI

Another time Nana visited me in Alaska, she smoked a cigarette. Again, she wore her red shawl. I always liked her in it. The shawl's mystique – partly aristocratic, partly uncanny – fit her well. She stood in the milky light of the midnight sun. Particles of dust rose and flittered like tiny angels in the flow that filled my room. Nana's skin was the color of alpenglow. Every night she woke me, I felt conflicting urges to cry and to laugh, to be a child ready to play and to be a confused adult unable to make sense of a reality that involved visiting spirits.

'You told me once that Alaska is so far away from home that it would dispel any illusion,' I said to her. 'I can't go any farther north. I don't understand. I have to make myself invisible to find myself, but I can barely see a shadow of who I am.'

Wisps of smoke drifted out of her lips and hovered above her like a personal heaven. This was proof that Nana's visitations weren't a product of my memory; Nana quit smoking long before I was born because she hated how the musty odor of tobacco stuck to her long after a cigarette. According to my mother, the months following her decision to quit were filled with complaints of deep-rooted cravings. My mother said she was quick to anger, forgot patience, and couldn't hold a conversation without moving her two empty fingers to her lips, teasing her mouth with a gesture that had become habit.

'Titi thinks I moved here to call attention to myself,' I continued as I followed Nana around my bedroom. 'As in, "Look at my dramatic escape." But that's not true, right?'

She opened drawers and closed them, peeked under my bed, and inspected my closet.

'Is Alaska just part of the illusion?' I asked.

I knew she wouldn't answer me – her spirit never spoke – but I half expected her to tell me what she was looking for.

'I have no audience, no reason for illusion,' I said.

She turned to face me. Ash fell from her cigarette, but before it reached the floor it turned into tiny gray butterflies that fluttered and vanished. Nana smiled the way she did when I solved one of her puzzles.

'How do I know reality in Alaska is any different than reality in Florida?'

She continued to smile, but this time it looked like amusement. I tried remembering how to ask the question in Spanish. The more I disappeared, the more things I did not know. At that moment, the only thing that was certain was Nana. I knew it was her and she no longer had to worry about the smell of cigarette smoke because she was a spirit, and spirits don't have to worry about such things.

When she exhaled, the air sparkled like sunlit snow. It took me a few minutes to realize that Nana never actually dragged the cigarette. She just held it between her steady fingers, the nails of which were painted the same color red as her shawl. The room filled with the smoke that passed through her, fogging the mirror attached to my dresser and clinging to the rotating fan blades. It didn't smell like anything was burning. Instead, there was the faint scent of something sweet.

*

The first few years in Orlando went according to plan. Instead of the large municipal clients my father had in Miami, he would now advise small businesses. Rather than living so far from home, Titi's first apartment was only minutes away. And the reorganization of my father's accounting practice promised my mother more time spent at home. With me. Despite all this, being hours from Nana meant I'd have to figure out my self-deceptive illusion on my own.

My father chose a new housing development called Hunters Creek. Almost every lot had a 'Sold' sign, but hardly any houses were built. I rode my bike past mounds of dirt and white sand, stacks of cement blocks, tractors churning the humid summer air. Their black gases became the only breeze. I used to ride to the end of the neighborhood, where tar-colored ponds cradled the banks of long green grass. I often noticed the sly eyes of an alligator peering above the oily surface or the sleek slivering body of a water moccasin carving S's into the marsh.

Once, I rode my bike straight over the hill and splashed into the pond. I sank, keeping just my nose and eyes above water like one of the gators. My hands remained fixed on the submerged handlebars while my feet kicked against the mushy ground. I waited like that for an hour, still among the hidden creatures. I wondered what it would be like to finally disappear. Maybe I wouldn't necessarily vanish. Maybe I'd transform into another life, like Nana's nightingales. While somewhere down the road my parents filed taxes in their new home, I considered the possibility that disappearing from one life could be an opportunity to reappear in another. Deep down, the thought of being so close to deadly beasts filled me with a fear I'd never before known, one that felt like hope.

For three years, I preferred the companionship of reptiles over the human kids at my new school. On occasion I brushed up against a good-sized gator that whipped me with its tail and then floated away. Other times a moccasin would lift its head out of the black water inches from my face, stare directly at me with a red glare in its sharp eyes, and duck back under. Anytime something like this happened, a paralyzing fear snapped through each of my joints, making me feel heavy and bloated in the water, but as the seconds passed without my moving, my taking a breath, I felt something I couldn't describe: Recognition? Understanding?

Still today, I have nightmares of those memories. In each one, either a snake or a gator comes close enough for me to hear its cold pulse. Stuck in the thick swamp, the grass ensnaring my feet, it watches me. All the snake has to do is bite. All the gator has to do is snap its open jaws shut. I wake up covered in a cold sweat, my legs kicking off the sheets I think are mud. The reptiles never strike, though, as if they see through my staged danger.

*

The summer I turned fourteen, I was riding home when someone yelled out to me. I turned and saw a tall, lanky kid running towards me. His body swayed as he ran, like the animated trees in a cartoon. I had never seen anyone in my neighborhood before. Though the houses had paint so fresh they smelled like a Home Depot, they were mostly empty. The windows remained dark and the walls silent. Not a single home where I lived was more than ten years old, but my neighborhood had that haunted feeling of loneliness.

This kid, who appeared my age, seemingly came from nowhere. He ran up to me, as if he would tackle me, but stopped a few inches short. 'Just this morning I caught a gator in that lake you always swim in,' he said.

'They don't bother me,' I said, wanting to sound tough.

'You from Florida?' He made wild shapes with his long arms. 'Anyone from Florida knows you don't enter a body of water deeper than your knees. You a thrill seeker or something?'

I turned back on my bike and started pedaling, but the kid easily lunged for the bar under my seat, grabbed it, and stopped me. 'I haven't seen you before,' he said. 'You going to Cypress Creek High School?'

'I guess so,' I said, staring at his flexed arm gripping my bike seat.

'You got more than gators to worry about.' He let go of my bike and pulled his shirt over his nose. 'You smell like shit.'

My clothes were soaked, clotted with grass and dirt.

'Do you think I was *in* danger?' I asked. 'Or is it just generally dangerous to swim in gator-filled lakes?'

'What's the difference?' He pinched his eyebrows and curled his lip.

'Do you know what my parents would say if they saw me in the lake? "Change out of your wet clothes before coming inside."'

He laughed and held his waist. Then, still smiling, he looked around, as if there was a chance we were being watched. Cookie-cutter homes all the same color mauve meandered into the distance. The only breaks in the pattern were the brown empty lots that hadn't yet been built. We were the only two people who could be seen.

'Do you know how to drive?' he asked, his grin adding an edge to his words.

I shook my head no. 'I'm only fourteen.'

'I'm at least older than that!'

'How old are you?'

'Fifteen.'

He stuck out his hand and introduced himself. He said his name was Dane, like the dog, and told me to meet him by the swamp that night. 'If you smell like reclaimed water, you're not getting in my car,' he said.

At 9pm sharp, Dane pulled up in a green Thunderbird Trans Am. He said it was his father's but he let him drive it whenever he wanted. We took turns pushing 90 mph down subdivision roads and the brightly lit streets on Disney property. The gravitational force pushing my heart against my spine and the unsettlingly likely prospect of death filled me with the same excitement as wading in reptile-infested ponds. When I explained this feeling to Dane, he said it sounded similar to the way his father described being drunk. So we decided to get drunk.

We paid a stranger outside of the liquor store to buy us a bottle of liquor with the highest percentage of alcohol. As Dane drove the backstreets behind Epcot Center, we took swigs from a bottle of Everclear. The surprisingly light liquid had the texture of a fire. It scalded my chest as it sloshed around inside my body traveling upwards to 160 mph. The danger so real, the act so believable, I couldn't get enough of this new fascination. In so many ways I had become intoxicated. This was a feeling far more powerful than what I felt wading in a lake. I could transform, rage against my own precious life. 'It's all about the scapegoat,' I said to Dane. 'The sacrifice!'

'What is?'

He turned into a cast member parking lot and spun the car in tight circles, hawk-like spirals that grew wider each rotation. The noxious odor of burning rubber clouded around us.

'Immolation!' I yelled out the open window.

'Fire!' he screamed.

'Martyrdom!'

'Death!'

A Disney security truck appeared and flashed its blue lights. Dane pulled over.

'What are you doing?' I asked, half laughing, half pissed that he'd give up so easily.

He looked at me with a seriousness that made him seem superior, wiser. 'Never run,' he said. 'Running implies guilt.'

The security guard, whose attempt to be threatening was belied by the smiling Mickey Mouse patch on his chest and shoulder, lectured Dane for his reckless driving. 'If I call the police, you'll have to pay a hefty ticket,' he said. His consoling voice made him appear way too kind to actually call the police. He sounded more like a guidance counselor.

As soon as the guard drove away, Dane floored it, spinning his tires and sending us wildly back onto the serpentine two-way road.

'Our only rule: never run,' Dane proudly reminded me.

Our easy escape disappointed me. Without understanding why, I knew the point *was* to get caught, *was* to be delivered shame-faced to my parents. 'Look what your son is doing to himself,' someone should say.

'Fucking rent-a-cop,' Dane said and passed me the Everclear bottle with one hand while gripping the steering wheel with his other. His tires squealed as we rounded a sharp turn.

When I felt sick, I kept drinking. When Dane told me to cool it, I kept drinking. And when he had to pull over so I could vomit and moan, I asked if I could have another sip.

'You're nuts,' he said, laughed, and hiccupped.

Around 3am he pulled into my driveway, carried me to the front door, rang the doorbell, and took off before anyone answered. My mom opened the door in jeans and a t-shirt, a phone in her hand.

'Where the hell have you been?'

My father appeared behind her, also dressed to go search the streets. No one was ready for bed in this house.

I leaned on the door frame and bowed my head, inside of which I heard applause.

'He's drunk,' my father said. 'Look what he's done to himself.'

I stumbled into the guest room and collapsed on the wicker couch, my mouth tasting like I'd been chewing on a cadaver.

'You said this wouldn't happen *in Orlando*,' my mom snorted.

'He smells like puke,' my father said.

As I floated in and out of a hot, painful consciousness, my mother wiped my face with a cool, damp cloth and repeated prayers. If I had any fluid left in me, I would have cried. If I had any power over time, I would have extended this moment forever.

I believe my parents thought moving to Orlando, with its close proximity to Walt Disney World, would somehow serve as therapy for me, as in, 'Here: pay attention to this illusion. Don't create your own anymore.' I don't know if it was irony or if Nana was just that much of a purist, but she detested the idea of me living in close proximity to Disney. Before we made the move, she told me, 'Don't go to that place. It will fill your mind with all sorts of fantasies and you'll never tell which way is up. A good magician should always know up from down.'

*

Dane already had the bag of weed given to him by his neighbor, a kid who designed skateboards and attended an alternative school. We skipped sixth period and sat in his Trans Am, passing the plastic bag of compacted pot back and forth. It felt firm and sticky in our hands. A warm scent, like very fine tea, could be squeezed from it. At first, we hadn't a clue how to actually smoke it. It was like we actually believed all we had to do was inhale the musty sweetness sealed in the plastic. Finally, Dane came up with the idea of shimming a cigarette and then stuffing it with the crumbled green flakes.

I expected the overpowering wave of drunkenness alcohol provided, the hot flash of illogical passion that reminded me of my parents' arguments. But I was disappointed by the subtlety of cannabis. I didn't want to simply relax. I wanted to feel myself erupt. I needed bravado and spectacle.

By the time Dane and I drove back to his house and sat in the cul-de-sac down the street, we came to the conclusion that pot was highly overrated.

We tried it again over the next couple of days, only because Dane insisted it was easier to drive around high than drunk. Over time, I came to appreciate the quiet introspection of being high. My vision felt clearer, sharper. Illusion made sense to me the way Nana explained it: I could see my condition; I could see Dane's condition. We were both accidents, exiles from our own lives. High, we didn't speed down streets serenaded with tinny Disney music. We didn't wail into the oppressive night. Instead, while Dane circled the city park, barely traveling at his car's neutral speed, he made a confession.

'My mother is sick,' he said. 'Like, really sick. But I don't know anything about it. My parents are keeping it a secret, as if I can't figure it out on my own.'

I felt a terrible onus to respond in some way that would validate Dane's painful crisis. Or a way that also felt like a concession on my behalf that his reality was realer than mine. His existence more memorable. Another Ginger.

'You want to drive down to Miami?' I asked.

'I can't go that far from home,' Dane said, and his voice sounded heavy with sadness. 'What if my mom has to go to the hospital? I don't want my dad taking her alone.'

The sullenness of Dane's voice carried a nostalgia that made me feel sick, the way banana smoothies reminded me of Barium. I hated Orlando, hated Florida. The entire state felt like an oblong stage on which I was always performing, always reminding myself and some imagined audience who I was. *I am* _____. Every time the blank filled with something different.

'What would you do in my situation?' Dane asked. The city's lights, trapped under ink-blotched clouds, reflected on the thin layer of moisture under Dane's eyes.

'Take flight,' I said. The humidity of late summer seemed to seal the sky against the ground.

The desire to know things I did not understand filled me with a great confusion, and I felt as though I could face those confusions more steadily with my mind numbed, the way anesthesia prepares the body for surgery.

I made Dane drive back to my house. The only consistent variable between alcohol and cannabis was my desire to get dropped off at home at the peak of my intoxication. I couldn't complete my high without a witness – namely, my mother or father. They had to know. They had to catch me. But I couldn't be the one to tell them, because then I would merely be a kid crying out for attention, and no one wants to read a story about that.

The entire way home Dane spoke of suspended shards of air, invisible to those who never considered breathing. I could see them. These shards hovered around my skin, perching on the blond hairs on my arm. Diamond dust, like glass crushed to powder, tickled my flesh. I checked myself in Dane's mirror and laughed at the size of my pupils, two galactic black holes floating in pools of red. Not the slightest ring of blue remained. My mind fixed on the possible reactions my parents would have when I walked inside reeking of pot.

I promised Dane I'd wait for him to drive away before opening the door and causing my scene. After the ecstatic engine hum of the Trans Am faded into the night, leaving behind the spurious quiet of the neighborhood, I rang the doorbell. It didn't matter that I had a key; I needed to signal my entrance.

My mother answered in her reading glasses, holding a book by Danielle Steel. Her presence gave off an orange aura that warmed me, lifted me. I felt lighter, pulled by the gravity of her existence. When my father appeared behind her, asking why I didn't open the door myself, the gravitational force galvanized and I couldn't imagine living without their curious stares to hold me together. To wonder at my every action. To come to their conclusions and to know.

In a motion that probably looked a lot like collapsing, I reached out and hugged my mother.

'He's drunk again.' My father: always the astute observer.

He helped my mother walk me to the guest room and lay me down on the wicker couch once more. This night, however, my mother did not stay with me applying cold compresses. She returned to cheap fiction, which, in many ways, was exactly what I did. My life was a formula – mishap and hyperbole. Through the door, I heard my father say, 'He smells like a skunk.'

I cried without knowing why. What surprised me more than the act of crying was the fear that my parents heard me cry. Wasn't the whole point to put on a show? Didn't I want them to know how badly I needed them? Instead, I buried my face in the sunflower-patterned pillow – each stitched thread biting into my skin – and cried. At some point in the night, I punched open the window in the guest room, set off the house alarm. The scramble of footsteps sounded overhead. They rushed down the stairs to disarm the control pad. In the meantime, I took a shard of glass in my already bloody hand and carved a vertical line down my left arm. Not deep enough to do any significant damage, of course. It was all for show.

The story I told my parents was that Dane needed serious help. I made up a story about him being depressed and suicidal. He was having a break-down, I lied. I wanted to hurry over to his house, but the window stuck. When I tried jamming it open it shattered. Of course, the story did not exonerate me from serious punishment, but at least I avoided their initial judgment: two months of seeing a psychiatrist.

My mother called Dane's father and told him about all the nights I'd come home drunk, with Dane as my driver. I was grounded; Dane was grounded. My mother drove me to school, picked me up from school, and never let me leave the house. Dane lost the Trans Am until he had an actual driver's license. Under indefinite lockdown, Dane and I met under our school's stadium bleachers to share a pot-stuffed cigarette.

While smoking, Dane considered quitting smoking.

'My mom's face turned completely white when she found out I drank alcohol,' he said. 'If she found out about this, God knows if she'd survive. If she gets worse because of me, I'd kill myself.'

I inhaled the dark, magic smoke and blew it in Dane's face. Then I fanned the smoke and apologized. 'We need to go to Miami,' I said. 'It's so much better than here.'

Dane's face turned red and he pushed me, hard enough so I stumbled. 'Did you hear me?'

I handed him the joint but didn't answer. Too much was implied in his question. Dane wanted to talk about his life in a way that made his pain remind me of my own. I spent time with Dane to flood my mind with a substance that did the complete opposite of remembering or being remembered. It was something like morphine for the forgotten. I didn't want to think about family secrets, obligations, or betrayals. In the smoke-clogged valves of my stoned heart, I believed this was the way to reverse the illusion: diving headlong right into it.

When my mother picked me up from school, I crawled around the backseat and barked, acting like our cocker spaniel, Ginger.

Later on that night, after a day of intermittent thunderstorms, my father came home and found me humping the living-room sofa.

'What's wrong with him now?' he asked my mother.

'He thinks he's a dog.'

'Isn't sixteen a bit old for this?' Behind each of my father's words was a cindering tone that threatened to burst from his mouth in a drizzle of hot embers.

'He's only fourteen,' my mother said. She rolled up some newspaper and smacked the floor.

Immediately, I dismounted the sofa and crawled in the space between it and the wall, whimpering.

'Oh. I'm so sorry,' my father said in his most sarcastic voice. 'Because it's completely normal for a fourteen-year-old to act like a dog.'

From behind the sofa, I could only see their feet – my mother in her open-toe slippers and my father in the black sneakers he tried to pass off as dress shoes. His legs were pillars of the earth. The ground sank where he stood.

'Well, you should at least know how old he is.'

My father huffed, sounding more exhausted than anything else.

*

We hadn't seen much of my sister since moving to Orlando, which completely went against the whole argument that we should live closer to her. She began working at Disney as a ride operator, pulling levers and pressing buttons that sent people splashing, spiraling, or soaring – depending on the ride – into some mechanical dream state. She began dating her manager, a bronze-skinned man much older than her, already with gray grizzle in his beard. She brought him over for dinner once, during which my father remained completely silent. No longer did my sister bring over girlfriends in neon spandex to dote over me like the ones in Miami did. As a fourteen-year-old boy, I would have welcomed that holdover, at the very least. But no. Instead, my sister disappeared into her life, one that put her in direct control of a captive audience. It was fitting, I always thought. Titi had always been skilled at manipulating whatever illusion was being performed, like when she showed up with bruised and battered Ginger, and then left her with us because her apartment allegedly did not allow dogs. By becoming a dog, I was able to fill multiple voids. My mother placed my dinner plate on the floor and let me scoop up the food with my mouth. Though my father hated when I did this, he let my mother continue to play along, all the while grumbling about how my behavior was 'crazy'.

Rest assured, the performance served a particular purpose. I hadn't the slightest clue, though, what that purpose was.

*

'Not that again,' my father said when he came home from work and found me on all fours, peeing in the backyard.

My mother held the sliding glass door open for me to crawl back inside. Playing this game high added a new level of entertainment. It pleased me no end to witness my mother's participation, as though she were another actor on my stage. Ginger, apparently aware of our implicit rivalry, wanted nothing to do with me. She hid under my mother's desk when I transformed. Sometimes, I'd hide under the desk with her – the two of us coiled into separate corners, divided by my mother's crossed feet.

From the first day my sister brought Ginger home, my mother adored the dog. Each morning she combed the thick knots out of her gold fur, cleaned her nappy ears with alcohol-dipped cotton balls. Each night, Ginger slept in bed with my parents, her body plopped over my mother's feet. I loved the way my mother loved that dog, but I hated Ginger for the same reason.

Somewhere, deep down, I knew how crazy it was for me to walk on all fours and bark when other kids my age skated past the house on rollerblades. I also knew how crazy it was for me to continue doing so despite my parents calling me crazy. They did not let me sleep in bed with them. I did not get my hair combed and ears cleaned the way Ginger did. All I got was a plate of food on the floor, served by my mother, while my father ordered me to sit in a chair like a human.

The culmination of my illusion came one night while my mother watched *Invasion of the Body Snatchers*. As she did during every horror movie she watched, she sat on the couch with her knees pressed against her chest, eyes wide in delicious fear. Usually, she barricaded herself with pillows, but this night, she called me up on the couch. I jumped up, sniffed the crumbs of peanut-buttered toast that sprang loose from the fabric, lapped a few into my mouth, and plopped down beside her. She held me against her body, her hand moist with nervous excitement grabbing strands of my fine, straight hair. She never had to comb the knots out. Never had to untangle it. Genetics disqualified me from that kind of treatment. My cheek pressed against her thigh, flexed tight with tension. I did not look at the TV, wanting to avoid spoiling the moment with images I knew would follow me into the night and twist my dreams into nightmares. Instead, I counted bald spots and impossible stains on the carpet, stared at the blur of spinning fan blades shaving the pale ceiling light. To ignore the screams and suspenseful music, I chewed on my palms, which itched from my walking on them all day. The movie, like reality, threatened to impregnate my mind with all sorts of horrors if I paid attention. And so I did dog things.

When my mother gasped during a particular scene, her arm squeezed my neck against her. I licked her knee to let her know it was okay. There were other horrors I wanted her to know. All I had to do was bark and yelp until my mother came running and scooped me up. She would know all on her own and I would be safe. Because I was a dog, I couldn't simply speak. That would have involved a suspension of disbelief that could have potentially compromised the success of the illusion altogether.

Ginger waddled by and noticed us. She stared first at my mother and then at me. She jumped up on the couch and lay on the other side of my mother. This was fine with me. Both Ginger and I were rescues.

No one knew the abuse Ginger took before her life with us. I closed my eyes and remembered the lesions and sores marking Ginger's shaved body. My relationship with Ginger was too complicated to simply call it envy. She deserved my mother's love and attention, but I was certain I did as well.

'Love me like the dog,' my illusion was trying to say.

I didn't have to ask anyone these questions because all I could do was bark, and when I barked those questions no one would understand. I could just chew my palms while my mother held me against her, as if protecting me from the hyper-real dangers projected on the TV.

*

Days when my parents left me home alone, Dane would ride his bike over to my house. We'd smoke on the patio, and almost against my will, as if instinct had taken over, I'd transform into a dog. Dane thought this was weird so he'd leave. If it was raining, Ginger and I would cower inside, staring at our reflections in the gray-soaked window. My parents knew how much Ginger hated getting wet, which made it difficult to take her out to go potty. Those days, I'd pee on the carpet in my father's office. Each time my father stepped in a puddle of urine in his office, Ginger was banned from sleeping on the bed for an undetermined number of days. Ginger was a good dog. She never chewed furniture, never begged at the table. The guilt I'd feel drove me to more heinous acts, like gnawing on my skin until I drew blood, wanting to harm myself as punishment for the injustice I committed.

I did feel a little better when, one day, my father asked my mother, 'How do you know *Ginger* is the one pissing and shitting inside the house all of a sudden?'

My mother stood in the kitchen, a bottle of Clorox in one hand and the rolled-up newspaper she smacked against the ground in the other. Her face blended confusion and impatience, as if my father had prompted her with a frustrating riddle.

'Don't forget,' my father said, 'now we have two stupid dogs.'

VII

One afternoon the next year, during a wet and windy May, my mother received a phone call from Nana's doctor in Miami, who informed her that Nana showed clear signs of dementia. According to the doctor, Nana needed someone to watch over her. A neighbor had to call fire rescue because she smelled burning coming from Nana's condo. It turned out she had left the stove burners on high and had stacked towels on top of them.

'Of course!' my father said when he heard the news. 'And now you want to move her to Orlando, so *we* can watch over her.'

'You act like the doctor is making this up,' my mother said.

'Maybe we should move out of Florida,' my father whispered, as if to himself. Then he locked himself in his study.

My mother looked into senior apartment homes near our house in Orlando and found one in Kissimmee that Nana could afford with her social security income. All the while, my father made the case that Nana had the sharpest mind and couldn't possibly have dementia. 'She can outwit all of us,' he said, and the desperation in his voice suggested he truly believed it.

The day my mother took Nana to visit Spring Hills Assisted Living, it was suitably rainy. 'I don't want to get wet and catch pneumonia,' Nana said. But my mother had learned resilience and insisted they go anyway.

They attended a tour of the facility and ate lunch in the dining room – crab cakes and spinach. After lunch, my mother walked Nana into a model room, furnished with a floral-patterned couch, a double bed that spanned a window with a view of the courtyard, a mini fridge, and a small TV.

'It's like a Quality Inn,' my mother said, her voice charged with ersatz showman excitement.

'Are you going to stay with me?' Nana asked. She lingered behind, keeping half her body out in the hall as if expecting a trap.

'You can't hurt yourself here. There will always be someone close by.'

My mother had only taken her eyes off Nana for a second, just to appraise the closet space, when she heard the avalanche-like sound, like a demolition. She spun around and saw Nana on the floor – the TV stand, and the TV on it, knocked over. Blood oozed from Nana's skull. She screamed, unable to form words, and hoped someone would interpret her scream as a call for help as she propped Nana up. A thin trail of blood trickled around Nana's nose and dripped down the edge of her grin.

'The carpet needs to be stretched,' Nana said. 'My foot stuck in one of its wrinkles.'

Finally, two nurses came running. They took Nana in a wheelchair to the health office. In the meantime, my mother insisted Nana could only have a room with tile floors. No carpeting whatsoever. Such a request, my mother was told, would put them on a three-month waiting list.

For the time being, Nana would get to stay with us at my parents' house.

Much later, my mother would tell my father and me that she went back and inspected the room. The carpet was as taut and new as a baby's skin, she would say.

*

Those days, Nana used the stove in our kitchen to make *palomilla*, *frijoles negros con arroz*, and *platanos maduros*. The house sizzled with the smell of olive oil snapping in the frying pan. She'd feed me, filling me with double the calories I'd just burned by jogging home from school.

'What time is my daughter coming home?' she often asked.

'She's never coming home,' I said. 'She has too many people to love.'

Nana looked at me with raised eyebrows, her face a mountain of sadness.

'Titi married her manager at It's a Small World. He has a nine-year-old daughter from a previous marriage. Now my sister's a mother. Mom's a grandmother. The dog's still alive.'

'*Ay, Dios mío*. No one told me Titi got married,' she said in a voice that had an equal amount of indignation and amazement.

'Technically, they aren't married,' I confessed. 'But they might as well be.'

'Do you know why her name is Titi and your name is Tito?'

'No.'

'*Mira*, my parents ran a chicken farm with some friends in Cuba. We called for the chickens by yelling, "Titi, Titi!" Tito was what we called the rooster. You are supposed to be the leader, but your mother loves Titi more than anyone else.'

'I thought the chicken farm thing happened in America,' I said, trying to hide how much her story hurt.

'It doesn't matter where.'

'I want to go to Cuba.'

Nana frowned and looked up at the ceiling. The whites in her eyes still brighter than pearls. It was one of the rare moments it felt like Nana was keeping a secret from me.

Later that night, my mother came into my room and asked if I told Nana some bogus story about Titi getting married.

'You know she's going to marry him,' I said. 'Her boss is her first real boyfriend.'

My mother's face changed. Sadness pulled at her cheeks. Her chin trembled. 'I asked Nana where she heard that story and she couldn't remember. She insisted I had told her before.'

This was supposed to be the payoff. The return. The climax to a successful two-act illusion completed by a legendary duo. I laughed, a nervous laugh that sounded more like panic than joy, and told her Nana and I were playing around.

'For as much as you love her,' she said, 'I'm stunned to see how you take advantage of her illness.'

She walked into her office, the sound of her footsteps lingering in the unlit hallway. I put down my book and walked out into the hall. Everything went dark after my mother closed her office door. To keep my bearings, I leaned against the door to the file room, which contained thousands of tax documents for various businesses. If Nana really had an illness, how did she time it so perfectly, have it work out to her benefit so precisely? Perhaps it was a genuine illness. She often stated that she looked forward to death. Usually, I attributed those comments to lower-level spells cast merely as an exercise, but she could have been telling the truth. To this day I think about a question Nana always asked me: 'Who is the crazier: the one who is so because he cannot help it, or the one who turns crazy of his own free will?'

I opened the door to my mother's office and said, 'Her mind will not respond to your reality. She lives in her own world. All we can do is enter it.' I felt my face getting hot with anger, as if my mother was the one who *took advantage* of Nana. As my voice grew louder, I felt older, more legitimate. I remembered my father, ready to burst from his suit while fighting with my mother. 'Every time you resist it, you confuse her. What are you going to gain arguing with her?' I felt very much like a villager from La Mancha.

All my mother did was stare at me, her ocean-green gaze as steady as the horizon out at sea, the white curls of her hair like cresting waves. My mother searched me for any semblance of sincere honesty. She knew she couldn't do it with words, tools of an apprentice illusionist. So she searched with her eyes, and found it. Deep down in the lockers of my soul's greatest depths I knew Nana was no longer in control. I knew I would lose her.

My mother held a finger to her lips. 'Don't yell,' she said. 'Let Nana sleep.'

*

When Nana moved into Spring Hills Assisted Living, my parents sold or donated most of her belongings. The only items Nana insisted she keep were her wigs. On the shelves behind her TV, Styrofoam busts displayed each wig: blonde and straight, maroon and bobbed, blue and spiked, black and curly, purple and long, orange and short. Nana would wear a different one depending on the situation. For instance, when she had to issue a maintenance request because her room was too cold, she matched her bobbed maroon wig with her gray pantsuit and marched to the front desk. The aura of a stern, managerial woman evidently radiated from her hair. 'Appearance is a powerful trick,' she said, smiling proudly once the maintenance workers left, the cold air no longer blowing out of the vents.

In Miami, I remember how her appearance was often part of her strategy. She wore a wig of black curls with a frumpy sweater when she demanded more weight loss pills from her doctor. She wore the long blonde wig with diced bangs when she took me to the movies and insisted on free candy and popcorn since the seats she wanted were already taken. Her plans always worked.

In Orlando, because she had given so much away already, I asked if I could have a wig.

'They can't do everything,' she said. 'I don't have a wig that would bring back my husband. I don't have a wig that would make my daughter want to spend more time with me. For those things to happen, I'd need to change my entire form. Become a ghost.'

After a few years living in Orlando, she would learn how to do just that, change her entire form. Become a ghost. She would sacrifice everything to do it – memory, health, life. Until that happened, though, it seemed her powers to alter her appearance depended on something as simple as a wig. When you're fifteen, you insist life is that simple.

*

One day in early June, I took my bike to Nana's. The sun filtered through purple-bellied clouds with flat bottoms and white puffy tops. The air was thick with a stillness that did not diffuse the exhaust of passing cars. When I reached Nana's apartment, the layers of sweat coating my body had the smell of spent gasoline.

Nana blended mamey with milk, and although the heat killed my thirst for dairy, I never turned down anything Nana made. We sat at her table, each of us with a glass of foaming rouged mamey. Her eyes had developed purple rings around them. Her hair had thinned like abandoned webs. Sunspots spread over her wrinkled skin. The only thing that remained as vivacious as always was her voice, steady and beautiful like the notes played by her organ.

'Where's your mother?' she asked, pushing the stacks of magazines on her table onto the floor. Clouds of dust rose like gun smoke and clung to the walls. There were candy wrappers and crumbs strewn all over. Dresses hung off the backs of chairs and the couch.

'She's at home with the maid,' I said. I loved how messy Nana's apartment was. No matter where she lived, her place reminded me of a jungle, someplace wild, a nice counter to my mother's pristine house, where everything was stored alphabetically in file cabinets. Instead of the plants she used to have, Nana's place now had the décor of a derelict.

'Always with the maid,' Nana said. 'I bet she only married your father because he's so organized.'

I asked Nana if she remembered the story of the nightingale. I wanted her to teach me Spanish. My mother didn't retain enough of the language to teach me and my father had forsaken his Spanish heritage completely. 'Spanish was a language,' as Nana said many years earlier, 'that could be shared only by the two of us.'

'If I could turn my daughter into a nightingale,' Nana said, her lips coated in mamey after taking a sip, 'I'd keep her in Pepe's old cage.'

As she recited the story in Spanish, making me repeat everything she said, I thought of my mother as a feathery bird with purple contours and a thin gray beak. Her cage would be spotless, shiny, and ordered.

'Will I ever become *el gran ilusionista*?' I asked.

Her answer, 'Read all of history.'

I asked Nana what else I could do.

'Read all of philosophy.'

What I needed to learn had to be somewhere in that Britannica set.

And so I read.

I started with Augustine. According to what the encyclopedia said about him, only when illusion was used for pleasure was it a sin. Marking Augustine's reference page was another card-sized note. The paper felt like powder in my hands. The note read: *No hay magia*. It was signed by Manny. Why wasn't there magic? I flipped through Volume A for another note, a continuation.

Aquinas's page had been dog-eared. I read about his claim that self-deception was the most deplorable act. I tried other volumes. I felt close to understanding why I was disappearing, why Manny disappeared. I felt close to something real. I didn't find any more notes from Manny, but I did read about Nietzsche's and Sartre's criticism of bad faith, which happened when we knowingly believed in illusions. I read some of Zeno's paradoxes, like the one about the indivisible quality of time and distance, rendering motion an illusion.

Nothing lined up. Some philosophers agreed with Manny's note. Others directly opposed what my grandfather wrote on the ancient paper as thin as dust. The more I read, the more I doubted I'd ever reverse the spell. It didn't matter that the spell was of a magic that may or may not have existed.

'Tell your mother I can be the maid,' Nana said before I left her apartment.

There were stacks of magazines in the kitchen sink, clothes spilling out of kitchen cabinets, and toothbrushes in a cup on her organ. How was all of that *not* magic?

On the way home, I spotted Dane's Trans Am parked at a gas station. I rode over just in time to catch him leaving the store and testing a newly purchased lighter. He saw me and stopped. 'It's okay,' I told him. 'I stopped turning into a dog.' He laughed and smoke seeped from his mouth. I chained my bike to a newspaper dispenser and got in his car. He had an apple with two holes poked in it.

'We can smoke out of fruit,' he said. 'It's healthier.'

We drove to the public park and crouched behind the baseball ditch. There, we tried out his apparatus. The smell of the smoke came out sweeter, milder. My sweat-dampened body made it easy for odors to stick to it, and with my source of power renewed, I transformed once again.

'At least you're not a dog anymore,' Dane said.

Quoting Nana, who liked to quote Don Quixote, I said, '*Yo se quien soy y se que puedo ser, si elijo.*'

Dane did not know Spanish. So I translated, 'I know who I am and who I may be, if I so choose.'

He had to think about it on the way back to the gas station, where my bike was chained. When I got out of his car, he said, 'Strange choice.'

With an eagerness that sent chills down my body despite the summer's heat, I pedaled home to show off my new form.

*

My father came home from work that night to find me wearing a white apron and mopping the tile floors. I then followed him into his bedroom, where I smoothed the wrinkles and creases out of the comforter, fluffed the pillows, and took his tie and jacket from him to hang in his closet. The entire time, he watched me with a suspicious eye, the way he watched hotel valets with his car key.

I served my parents their dinner, ate my own in the kitchen, and then collected their plates when they finished. Each time my father would start explaining work details, he'd stop himself and stare at me, his face expressing something between disgust and disbelief. My mother remarked how nice I'd been all day.

That same night, when my father found me in his closet, he called my mother into the room. 'Why is the dog polishing my shoes at 10pm?'

'He's not the dog anymore,' my mother said. She leaned against the closet door, watching me with a faint smile, a subtle pride that all mothers should feel towards their sons. 'He's the maid.'

'Of course,' my father said, sighed. 'I'm always the last to know anything.'

VIII

Each time one of us chucked a rock from the roof of the Hilton, we'd listen with suspended delight for the shatter of glass. The bust of aluminum also satisfied us, but not as much as that drizzling sound, crystal rain splattering on cement. Twenty stories below, no parked car was safe. It took security thirty minutes to notice we'd snuck up the hotel's stairwell. But it would only take us five minutes to talk our way out of trouble.

Never run.

The wind carried the rocks we tossed. Despite their density, they'd swirl and spin onto new trajectories, as if fate took control of each rock moments before it crashed into metal and glass.

Dane spun a pebble in his palm, staring at it through dark sunglasses. Strong gusts would knock him back a step, but he was otherwise a statue. For the last few minutes, I'd been the only one chucking.

'Are you done?' I asked.

'I found out it's lung cancer,' he said. He wore his sunglasses. The deep night sky would soon erupt in Disney's nightly fireworks, but the sunglasses seemed unnecessary.

'It's a rock,' I said, and threw the one I was holding. It pummeled the air, ricocheted off wind, and crashed into a Buick.

'I found my mother's living will. She still doesn't know I know. I'm going to be eighteen soon, an adult, but my parents think I'm too much of a child to understand.'

'Understand what?' I snapped. My voice rang with irritation. I didn't want to talk about this. Not now. This wasn't why I was here. I dropped the rock I was holding. There was no point in throwing it anymore.

'My mother's dying,' Dane said and pitched the pebble at my feet. I hopped over it. 'Goddamn it, Tito.'

He grabbed his head with both hands and turned his back to me. I did not like feeling implicated. After all, I had nothing to do with his mother's health. If Dane chose to confess his family's secrets, that was his prerogative. There was no way I'd do the same. As I convinced myself of this, I thought of my parents' late-night arguments. Here they were all over again. My imagined drama once again gave way to real life tragedy. My story was a melodrama in comparison. I needed tragedy – a bloody nose, an eating disorder, a dying grandmother.

Our shirts whipped around our thin bodies like flags tangled on their poles. But something else happened. I felt the wind like I'd never felt it before. It didn't just whip around me, it howled *through* me. It lifted me, somehow, off my feet.

It carried me.

I couldn't be sure how far I'd moved, if I did at all. I became dizzy and disoriented.

Dane turned around and stared at me. When he tore off his sunglasses, I expected to see rage in his eyes. Instead, they only showed fear. His mouth hung open as if trying to swallow the wind. 'How did you do that?' he asked.

'Do what?' I was getting impatient. Hotel security took far too long this time to catch us, call our parents, and threaten us with juvenile detention. Prison would have been preferable. Anything other than facing our all-too-clear histories.

'Your skin,' he said, and went silent. He dropped his glasses and reached out to grab me. He held up my forearm like a beacon. A gust of wind rushed over Dane but passed through my arm. My bones chilled. Within the second it took for the gust to pass us, my arm vanished. And when the wind settled, my arm returned. It was fast, easy to miss without someone paying close attention. My body flickered like a candle. Any breeze blew my essence out. In Dane's eyes, I had to imagine, I'd become just shorts and a shirt.

In the indigo distance, fireworks lit up the sky. Blasts of green, red, and yellow reflected off my translucent skin. He asked if I felt okay, but before I could answer he pulled me back inside the stairwell and punched me in the stomach. 'Still solid,' he said.

Several flights of stairs below, the metal door swung open and clanged against the wall. A herd of footsteps caromed up the well. There could have been five, maybe six, security guards coming for us. Dane and I ran into the hallway, running by hotel room doors as the fireworks thundered outside.

'You don't give a shit about anyone but yourself,' he said while running. 'This is serious. It is not TV.'

I wanted to stop, let security get me. But that would have proven Dane right.

We took the main elevator, breathing heavily as a man and woman kept their two children huddled close to them. The family of four stared at us like we were unpredictable animals, savage and hungry. The moment the elevator reached the lobby and the doors slid open we took off. We ran, breaking our rule, which was to never run.

Running implied guilt.

But it was too late for us to do anything else. We didn't just run from security. We ran from lives we couldn't understand, no matter how much we made ourselves miserable trying. We ran from a disappearing mother and a disappearing self. Outside, it sounded like the entire world was under siege. Everything was shattering. Rocks rained down on all of us.

The next day at school, Dane told students in Algebra II that I could turn invisible. Coach Showalter, our teacher, laughed and said, 'He should learn to turn himself invisible on test days then.'

I leaned over to Dane. 'Fuck you,' I whispered. 'It's not real.'

Dane wore a smile I didn't recognize. The corners of his mouth now had a slight inward curl. His cheeks squeezed too hard, it seemed, as if some tension were ready to erupt from behind his gritted teeth.

He rubbed my shoulder, and then turned back to the red-headed girl who sat behind me. She had her feet on her skateboard and was rolling it into the legs of my seat.

'Touch his shoulder,' he told her. 'It's like nothing is there.'

'Don't listen to him,' I warned. 'He thinks this class is called Algebra II because he failed it the first time.'

'It's his headline act: bad jokes and then poof, gone,' Dane said, his wicked smirk adding a hiss to his words. 'Ladies and gentlemen, witness, if you can *see* him, the incredible invisible Tito!'

'That's enough, Dane,' Coach Showalter said, smiling in apparent amusement.

'It could be he weighs like forty pounds,' the girl said. She poked me in the shoulder with her finger. 'You'd be like my little sister.'

I waited until class let out and we were in the hall. Students rushed by us like an undercurrent, trying to pull us out to sea. My feet did not feel steady. 'Maybe you'll get lung cancer like your mom,' I said. 'Then *you* can have center stage.'

Dane stood square in front of me, as resolute as he was on the top of the Hilton with the wind pushing against him. Nothing moved him.

I shoved him hard against the lockers. They made that loud metal crackle that echoed down the hall. I lost my balance and fell against him. Our bodies tangled as we fell to the floor. I had his leg in my arms. He had my head wrenched under his armpit. I mostly heard laughter from the students around us. It probably didn't look much like a fight.

When Coach Showalter pulled us apart, he scowled at me. 'Jesus, Tito,' he said. He bent over with his hands on his knees, gasping for air. It looked like he was the one in the fight. Once Coach Showalter caught his breath, he asked, 'Can't you take a joke?'

*

Nana was writing down memories in her notebook. *Called Penny at noon. She's busy working until five. Call her at five.* The doctor recommended this activity. My mother mandated it. Each time Nana called my mother and asked her to come over, Nana had to recite a full page from her memory book. If she couldn't do it, my mother did not come over. Her love was always the reward.

A show about people stranded on an island played on the TV. A large man in a threadbare blue shirt bowled through trees. He was chasing a much skinnier man in red. 'When I get my hands on you...' the man in pursuit threatened.

I stripped out of the long-sleeved windbreaker I'd started wearing. While this prevented the wind from blowing my body away, I melted inside the outfit. The material trapped the heat inside. My face glistened all day with sweat.

In just my shorts and t-shirt, I splashed water over my arms and legs. My legs were gone. In the mirror, I saw only socks and shoes. My left hand faded in and out like an old TV screen. I could see only splotches of my face and neck. I showed Nana and she said, 'Why were you wearing such a funny outfit?'

The windbreaker was a reflective lime green with sky blue pinstripes. It would have been offensive even to someone who was color-blind.

'You looked like Pepe.'

Nana laughed, amused, and then returned to her memory book.

'Can I borrow some of your memories?' she asked. 'I don't have enough.'

On the TV, the man in red burst into a hut and asked the woman inside to hide him. 'He wants to kill me for giving him amnesia,' the man in red said. A few seconds later, the larger man, panting, knocked on the door to the hut. The woman answered in a sparkling black dress that contrasted the dilapidated hut. She leaned against the panting, fuming man, tickled his chin and rubbed his fat belly. While she flirted with him, the wily man in red opened the back window and tried climbing out.

I closed the blinds on Nana's window and sat next to her. Rubbing my hands together seemed to revitalize my arms. I was now at least murky.

Nana had memories scrawled in all directions in her book. *Had chocolate for breakfast. Donde estan mis dientes.* There was no discernable sequence or design to her memories. She wrote *Tito dressed like Pepe* immediately after *General Hospital – channel 10*. Without a clear narrative, Nana wouldn't get to spend time with my mother.

'I think I'm losing control,' I said, quick and without internal rehearsal. I feared disappointing Nana. This was, after all, her art, which she spent years practicing. And I misused it.

'Terry next door is baking,' she said. The smell of buttermilk biscuits floated in the air. Nana's jaw trembled as if she were already chewing one. 'Let me show you off, Tito-my-love. Maybe she'll give us some.'

'I'm not really hungry.'

'I'm the only person who gets visitors here. It makes everyone jealous when you and your mother come by.' She smiled brilliantly. Despite her disheveled hair and twisted nightgown, she displayed an aristocratic beauty. 'You should eat, anyway. You're losing weight.'

Hearing Nana say that embarrassed me, much more than Dane's teasing or Coach Showalter's chiding. I looked away from Nana at the picture frames of her with my mother as a child. In each picture, my mother, held by Nana, smiled. In fact, there wasn't one picture of my mother alone without Nana carrying, holding, touching, or hugging her. Always possessed. Always smiling.

The man in red of course knocked over the woman's dresser trying to climb out the back window. The ruckus snapped his pursuer out of the flirty trance.

Fed Pepe II, Nana wrote in her memory book. I told her she didn't have any Pepe anymore, so she asked me who she fed this morning.

'Please help me.' I wanted to cry, but this was supposed to be Nana's proud moment. She had a visitor.

'*Pobrecito*,' she said, held my hand. Her frail fingers felt like they would turn to dust in my grip. '*Escúchame*. Before the revolution, not many in Cuba knew Yúcahu's story. *Pero* after, so many people began transforming into these beautiful birds, flying out into the sea. The families of those who flew into the horizon remained on the shore, stranded because they did not know magic. They cried, prayed. They were heartbroken, but grateful that at least someone in the family knew the story.'

'I thought you hated the revolution.'

'No. I hate the outcome.'

'I don't understand.'

'I tell you. It only makes sense in Spanish.' Nana stood up and straightened her gown. When she did so, the pansies printed on her gown seemed to flutter around her, as if Nana stood in a spring meadow.

'What am I supposed to do?'

'Let me get dressed so we can get some of those biscuits.'

'None of my teachers ever talk about the Cuban Revolution.'

Nana sat back down, the pansies settling on her lap. She sucked in her lips and stared at me, her eyes wet with pity. 'Cuba had many problems,' she said. 'The government before the revolution was terrible. It saved all the money for foreigners, treating Cubans like slaves. Manny was one of the people calling for change. But what happened was not freedom. It was just an illusion.'

It still didn't make sense to me. I flipped through Nana's memory book, half expecting to find some answer buried within the random notes – *Titi married man with daughter. Manny left for Cuba. Miami is now Orlando.* Beyond all logic, I tried convincing myself that the entire notebook was a puzzle Nana had devised solely for this purpose. *Flushed toilet. Tell Penny about the leak. Rain for thirty minutes.* All of it could have been a cryptic guide that, once deciphered, would clarify everything and save me from my wanton practice of this dangerous art.

The big blue man finally caught the scrawny red man, who was readying a rowboat to leave the island.

'Don't worry, Little Buddy,' he said as he grabbed a handful of red shirt and lifted the branch-sized body out of the rowboat. 'You won't remember the pain once *I* knock amnesia into *you*.'

'You don't understand,' he pleaded, kicking for the ground. 'We have this amnesia thing all wrong, from a phenomenological perspective anyway. Think about it. Several pre-Christian societies established festivals celebrating a willful forgetting of the self in society, such as Saturnalia in ancient Rome, Bacchanalia in ancient Greece, and similar Lord of Misrule rituals in Mesopotamia. During these festivals, commoners, peasants, and fools were publicly elected to preside over the carnivalesque holiday functions. In effect, they became public officials. Women and lower clergy and slaves reversed their fixed fate and enjoyed a day of rule over the imperial hierarchs, who acted as plebians. The lords of misrule performed ceremonies that *parodied* the actual, sacred events. When Christianity was introduced, the French *societies joyeuses* included mock sermons panegyrizing the lives of imaginary saints. Forgetting isn't loss, Skip. It's remembering what can be imagined.'

The anger in the man's face faded, and he let go of the skinnier man. His white eyebrows formed snowy slopes on his forehead. He appeared far too sad for the tone of the show. He looked confused, depressed, drugged. 'If it's all a lie, why remember at all?' he said.

'Our source of pain is remembering the main-land,' the man in red said and pointed somewhere at the studio-painted horizon. 'Erasmus's *Folly* suggests that illusion occurs whenever a certain pleasant mental distraction relieves the heart from its anxieties and cares, and at the same time soothes it with the balm of manifold pleasures.'

'I still have my sense of smell,' Nana said, smiling. She stood up again and raised her nose in the air, taking in the biscuits' buttery aroma.

Just before I decided to give up, close the memory book and follow Nana out to Terry's apartment, I saw it. The broad sweeps of cursive formed bubbled letters much clearer than the typical scribbles. Scrawled diagonally, catawampus to the other notes, observations, reminders, was the message: *Leave the birdcage and window open.*

IX

My father brought a pair of pants for Nana to hem, which my mother carried into Nana's room. He dug around in Nana's storage closet and withdrew her old sewing machine. Nana was slouched in her recliner, staring at the flashing TV screen. Her eyes reflected the images. When I first saw her, I was terrified. There didn't seem to be anything behind the reflections.

'These jobs will keep her alive,' my father said, clapping with excitement once he got the sewing machine plugged in.

'I'm worried about her using that,' my mother whispered.

Nana sucked her teeth so hard they almost fell out. She waved her hands like she was surrendering. 'I guess I'm an imbecile,' she quipped.

All of her years, memories, spectacle, and brilliance returned to her eyes and I felt better.

My father smiled and hugged her. 'That's the mother-in-law I know,' he said. 'You always have a hat of tricks.'

He handed her the pants and set the sewing machine on the table. As he plugged it into the wall, Nana traced her finger down the seam of his pants. When she reached the trim, she looked up at my mother in confusion. Her face suggested she was lost, worried, even scared.

My mother sat on the couch and held Nana's hands. She looked at the carpet, the wall, her own feet with toes pointed in, and then at me. My mother seemed ready to break into little pieces, as if only a single thread held her together.

I went into Nana's bedroom so no one would see me cry. But I couldn't actually cry. It was a feeling like dry heaving, a sickness that isn't really a sickness. Nothing feels as nauseating as teetering on the edge of reality.

I crawled under Nana's bed, wedged my body between the suitcases and storage boxes she kept. This I learned from my dog days – to find a den during moments of distress. Dust rose from the carpet and irritated my eyes. Everything became blurry. I breathed in the odor of old shoes, of ancient books with yellowed pages, and fallen trees about to rot.

I rubbed my eyes and pulled the collar of my shirt up over my nose and mouth. With my vision somewhat normal, I noticed a slip of paper trapped in the lid of a shoebox. Another note from Manny!

The voices from the living room washed away. The tunneled silence gave way for the Spanish I tried translating.

You have to leave home to know you exist. But if you don't go far enough, the sun will remind you of Cuba and you'll die of homesickness. There's no snow in Florida. Go to Alaska.

My father clapped his hands and the sound was like thunder tearing apart the sky. I sprang, banged my head against the bed frame.

'All set up,' he said.

I crawled back out and met my parents in the living room.

'Did Manny ever go to Alaska?' I asked Nana. She looked at me with blank eyes, like I'd been telling her how to use the sewing machine.

'No,' my mother said, laughing. 'That's too cold for his Cuban blood.'

My father held Nana's shoulder to call her attention back to him. He told her, 'When you finish, I'll bring the shredder. I have a lot of documents that need shredding.' Something in my father looked fragile, like he was at the edge of tears, laughter, or both. He held onto Nana, and I had the sense he couldn't let go no matter how much he wanted to.

After we left, my parents sat silently in the car before starting the engine. I could feel their worry, their fear that something was wrong with Nana. I squeezed Manny's note in the palm of my hand, like it contained the answer everyone needed to survive.

*

For the remainder of high school, I came straight home each day, stripped out of the parakeet-colored windbreakers hiding my vanishing body, and input clients' cash receipts for my father. With the money he paid me, I bought books. I spent days in libraries and used bookstores. I insisted on only reading books that had been already read by others. Despite how impossible it sounded, I held onto the belief that I'd come across another note from Manny. In each used book, I tried feeling for a previous life. I closed my eyes, thumbed the fibrous texture of the pages and listened for something familiar. Nana's memory grew worse and I steadily disappeared. Any sign would have been, at least, something.

In the meantime, I sought books specifically about illusion. As it turned out, *all* books are about illusion. Consider the following examples:

The Bible warns of man's inherent desire to be deceived by illusion.

The *Bhagavad Gita* shows how man can overcome his desire for illusion.

The poetry of Rumi provides examples of a life balanced by reality and illusion.

Plato's *Republic* claims those who only know shadows will murder the man who tries exposing their illusion.

The philosophy of Jean-Paul Sartre blames societal pressure for our bad faith in illusions.

Everywhere I looked, I found at least a sentence postulating our relationship with magic. It seemed the only reason one wrote anything at all. I took notes. I annotated. I compared works and imagined conversations between the authors. While this didn't necessarily clear up my particular predicament, it did set me on a path of sorts.

The summer following my graduation, I began planning my move to Alaska.

'Alaska,' my dad said after I informed my parents of my plans. 'Maybe you can get a job as a sled dog.'

That joke was years late.

*

Just before Thanksgiving, the last I'd spend in Florida, Titi married her boyfriend, the manager of It's a Small World, for real this time. The wedding took place in his backyard. Now, she lived with him and his teenage daughter.

They all arrived together for Thanksgiving, my sister part of a new family, showing up with a sweet potato casserole as if they were merely guests, neighbors, outsiders. Her husband greeted me with a high five, and then pretty much ignored my presence the entire night. Pupi, my sister's new daughter, carried an edge about her, like she didn't really trust any of us.

'You'd like my brother,' Titi said when she introduced us. 'He wants to move to Alaska.'

'Does he?' Pupi blended just a hint of sarcasm in her question so that it could reasonably pass as genuine interest. Her suspicion of us seemed to include Titi.

My mother ate the entire sweet potato casserole, baked with three marshmallow layers, and drank two bottles of eggnog, one of them with rum.

A week later, while she and I watched a French film about World War I, she opened a brand-new pack of Oreos. Thirty minutes into the movie, she had eaten all forty-five cookies. I watched her chew every single cream-filled sandwich, and then pick off the chocolate crumbs from her lap and eat those, too. The way she did it, with eyes wide open in suspense as she brought each Oreo up over her head and down to her mouth, made it difficult to tell the movie apart from real life.

My mother sucked the crumbs clinging to her fingers. Then she said to me, 'You missed out on a good dessert.'

I had been raised by Nana long enough to detect bravado. This was an act. I couldn't stand thinking that my mother needed an audience. *She* was the audience. *She* was the purpose for everyone's illusion. Nana wanted an obedient daughter. I wanted a devoted mother. And now she wanted...

What? And would she end up like Nana and me, doomed by our own spells?

One French soldier asked another if he remembered what that troublemaking islander said about Erasmus.

The other French soldier shrugged.

The first soldier said, 'There is no difference between those in Plato's imaginary cave that stand gaping at the shadows and figures of things, so they please themselves and have no need to wish, and that wise man, who, got loose from them, sees things truly as they are.' Gunfire ripped through the blue fog above them. Pebbles tumbled down the trench walls. 'And if there is a difference: those in the cave have the advantage. First, in that their happiness costs them least, that is to say, only some small persuasion; next, that they enjoy it in common.'

The other soldier slapped him on the chest. 'I get it,' he said. 'The Germans. Christmas Day.' Then the soldier reached beyond the TV screen for an Oreo and, realizing my mother had eaten them all, became irritated. 'Really?' he asked, tapping his rifle against the ground. 'All of them?'

Later that night, after my mother had gone to bed, I investigated the pantry. I found dozens of opened cookie packages, cans of soda, individually wrapped cakes, bite-sized Kit-Kats. The place was a sugar stronghold.

*

On Christmas Eve, my mother accepted a tin container of various cookies from a neighbor. Macaroons, moon pies, half-moons, sugar biscuits, cranberry scones, and Russian tea cakes. My mother took the container to her office, a dark corner of the house. To the best of all our abilities, we wanted to pretend this was a home and only a home, so on holidays most of the family avoided any room with file cabinets and copy machines.

Every hour or so, my mother slipped backstage, out of her beloved audience's sight, and swallowed dessert. By Christmas morning, all the cookies were gone. According to the neighbor, she had made more than fifty.

From the couch, where I sat with Nana, I watched as my mother ran from one side of the house to the other. In the rare moments she stood in one place, she tapped her toe or swung her arms. Her face grew Christmas red. Her static stare couldn't seem to focus on anything. When serving the prime rib she'd spent all day cooking, her hands shook, splattering gravy all over the white counter and tiles.

Nana whispered to me, 'Your mother has the spell.'

Just as she said that, my mother dropped a plate on the floor. Ceramic shattered, silencing the conversations between uncles and sisters and fathers. My mother waved her hands in the air, like a conductor that signaled the uproar of laughter.

I stayed seated on the couch, with my back to Nana so I could continue watching my mother's frenetic spurts.

'*Ay*, you have to help her,' Nana said.

'How?'

'Find out what spell she's cast on herself. Don't let it become irreversible.'

I could feel Nana's fingers playing the organ on my spine, the way she used to put me to sleep as a child. The notes vibrated up and down my back, sounding so far away.

A few days after the New Year, Titi cornered me. She ripped open my windbreaker jacket, revealing my translucent shoulder.

'What's going on?' she asked, sounding more irritated than concerned.

I shrugged free of her grip – something I've never been able to do before – and zipped up the jacket.

Since Titi got married, something in her softened. She seemed more uncertain about her life. The mature confidence of her teenage years had become a cautious reserve.

'Come with me to Pupi's dance,' she said. Even her request sounded more like a question than a demand, which I wasn't used to. This new change in tone caught me off guard, so I agreed.

The dance show took place in Celebration, a neighborhood designed by Disney to be a combination of Victorian architecture and Key West color schemes. During holiday shows such as this one, which took place on a rollaway stage set in Celebration's Main Street, machines fixed to light poles spewed fake snow. The Floridians went wild, making snow angels on the soapy pavement.

In Orlando, facades are very important.

She pulled me after her through crowds of women in sweaters, of adolescent girls in sparkling skirts and black tights, and of men aiming a camera at the stage with one hand and holding a bottle of beer with the other. It all seemed too neat, the way a neighborhood designed by Disney would seem. The presentation was too slick, the experience too predictable. I understood why Nana hated Disney so much. 'They are an illusion of an illusion,' she had said. 'Magic is supposed to make it easier to understand what is real, but for Disney, magic confuses what is real.'

Titi found us seats in the front row, which was way too close to the stage. In the first act, a dancing toddler almost mule-kicked me.

'I set all this up,' Titi said and waved at some people across the stage.

My sister had grown thin. She had the tired look of a woman who lived a life of routine. Her hair was now greasy and always back in a ponytail. Her loose shirt dangled on her shoulders and had stains on the chest.

'I made all the arrangements with City Hall,' she said, squeezing my arm.

I looked down, making sure I still had an arm to squeeze.

'I walked into each café and shop on this street, petitioning support.'

'Support?'

'Starbucks is offering free hot chocolate. Woofgang Pucks is offering free dog treats. There's a keychain giveaway. The dance company wouldn't have an audience tonight if it weren't for me. This is *my* audience.'

The more she spoke, the more intent her stare became, as if she was searching for some very important piece of evidence, the single most valuable datum she wanted to show me. Her eyebrows pushed up her forehead's skin and her fingers dug into my arm.

The turnout was impressive. Parking was a nightmare. The small-town charm Celebration promised had become an outright lie, to Titi's benefit. She had also coordinated everything without missing work. Working for Disney isn't exactly a high-paying career, so neither she nor her husband could afford to take time off. In the past few years, she'd moved up from It's a Small World ride operator to private tour guide.

'Pupi's group is up,' Titi said. My niece trotted onto the stage, leading a gaggle of pre-teens in tights. 'Watch how she never loses her smile. That's what I taught her. No matter what, keep the crowd smiling back.'

The deep bass of some hip-hop song pounded the speakers. The street thumped. My niece danced and, as my sister promised, smiled.

After it was all over, we went to the Market Street Café. Also to my sister's credit, the café offered free milkshakes to dancers and their families. While we were there, my mother called my phone, asking when I was coming home.

'She cares more about you than she does me,' Titi said. 'Ever since your talk of moving to Alaska, she's become obsessed with you.'

Pupi chugged her chocolate shake in one continuous sip, only stopping to take a breath. Still, she didn't remove her lips from the straw. I told her it was as though she hadn't eaten all day.

'I haven't,' she said. She had metallic eye shadow that gave her face the shine of a newly painted car. Her lipstick was emergency red. My niece was also thin. With her hair sprayed and pulled back into a bun, she looked like a plastic doll that a normal-sized kid could play with.

'Let's tease Mom,' Titi said. She took my phone and sent a text message that read: 'Tito got drunk and took off. He's back to his old ways.'

Right away I felt uncomfortable. I had no idea what was happening, but it felt nostalgic, like those years I spent trying to break the world, but instead of having Dane by my side, I had my sister. I wasn't sure how to regard Titi: partner or competitor?

It didn't take two minutes for my mother to call my cell phone, which Titi answered. 'Yeah... I don't know... All I said was he should realize he won't be happy anywhere so why leave Florida...' She winked at me, a wink that felt incisively ironic. 'Then he threw his phone down and stormed off...'

Not until her milkshake was finished did Pupi pay any attention to us. 'I can see through you,' she told me, taking deep, sweet, sticky breaths.

'Your mom's getting me in trouble with my mom,' I said.

Titi handed my phone back to me with a tight-lipped grin, as if she had just heard a secret that had the potential of becoming a very good rumor.

Instead of calling my phone again, my mother called Titi's phone. Her face darkened when she answered. She hung her head, hiding behind her hair, looking embarrassed, ashamed. 'It's a joke,' she said. 'He's right here. Talk to him.' As she handed me her phone, she stuck out her bottom lip. Her eyebrows formed a pyramid.

What could I do?

My mother was hysterical, crying as if she had the wind knocked out of her. 'Why are you leaving?' she said. 'Oh God, why?'

'It was a joke.'

'It's not a joke. Why can't you go to college in Florida?' The phone crackled with static every time she gasped for the air she desperately needed.

On the way home, Titi swore Mom hadn't been acting out of the ordinary. 'It's been hard for her to watch Nana get worse. She's doing the best she can, but she's still the same Mom you used to play tricks on.'

'I don't play tricks,' I said.

Titi sighed, stared straight ahead for a moment before saying, 'When you were going around getting wasted, Mom used to call me crying – in hysterics! She thought you were trying to kill yourself.'

'Do you know what I found in the pantry? She's bingeing on shit food, which she's never done before. This entire family plays tricks!'

She slammed on the brakes at a green light. The car behind us honked, then swerved around us. Titi sat there until the light turned yellow, and finally red.

'*You're* the illusionist,' she said and slapped my chest. There was so much anger packed into her voice I wondered how long she'd wanted to say exactly that.

I looked in the backseat. Fortunately, Pupi had fallen asleep.

'I've spent my whole life here, plain as day for everyone to see. I'll probably never leave Florida. But you? You are becoming invisible.'

The light turned green and I pointed ahead, but my sister kept the car planted at the intersection. Cars behind her honked, drivers cursed. The flow of traffic washed around us in a current that couldn't budge us.

'*Look* at my life,' Titi said. 'I married my boss, like Mom married her boss. I have a daughter who prefers her *real* mother. The one thing I look forward to is coordinating a community dance concert. My life is just as unimportant as yours, but I don't need applause. Sure, I don't feel as loved as I think I should feel, but I'm not running to fucking *Alaska*.'

She waited until the light turned red for the third time to cross the intersection. I closed my eyes and imagined the impact of another car slamming into the passenger side. That, too, would have been too predictable.

'Why don't *you* stop the illusion?' Titi asked, her words heavy with years of unspoken judgment.

After a trip that seemed to last my entire life, she finally pulled into the driveway. Before I could get out, she grabbed my arm. I saw her years then. She was no longer a glitter-splattered made-for-TV teen. She looked far older than someone in her mid-twenties.

Her skin stretched thin over her cheekbones. The shadows under her eyes looked like deep stains left by tears.

'Nana is really sick,' she said. I felt light enough to float away. It was like Titi sensed that feeling and tightened her grip on my arm. 'Not like some invisibility spell. But *really* sick. You of all people should know. You are her best friend.'

I nodded, and she let go.

When I entered the house, I felt overcome with nostalgia, a sick feeling of familiarity, of longing for a life already lived. I remembered coming home drunk, or drugged, and trudging past my parents for the guest bedroom. Of course, the night I finally arrived sober was the most painful one.

I found my mother crying into my father's shoulder, the two of them sitting on the maroon leather couch in the living room. An animated Christmas movie played on the TV. She hated animation. *It's not real*, she always claimed.

'You really did a number on her,' my father said, looking at me with sharp disapproval, the look he always had when he told my mother that I was drunk.

'I didn't do or say anything.'

'You will,' my mother said in between sobs. 'You are leaving.'

I thought of Nana then – her driving her white Accord into the parent loop to pick me up from school; her yelling in Spanish at the TV; her playing the organ, singing in a rhythm slightly behind the tune.

The animated train conductor had just handed the young boy his punched ticket to return home. Santa and the elves stood behind the conductor. They were still cheering. The conductor said to the young boy, 'Yet I ask you to look at the wooden puppets, worn out by their moment of play on the stage.' I didn't understand what Christmas had to do with Han-Shan.

My father turned off the TV. 'Pay attention to what's going on here,' he said. 'Stop tuning the world out.'

'If I don't leave Florida, I'll never become anything.' I wasn't really sure what to say. Being forced to address everything so suddenly made my mind as blank as the TV now was.

My parents didn't respond. My mother, at least, calmed down a bit. Her face remained buried in my father's brown collared shirt as her arms lay limp in her own lap. Wasn't this everything I wanted – a grandstand display of how much I was loved and therefore should not move across the continent? Nothing felt right. The emptiness of air spilled into and out of me. Something was missing, and not just various parts of my body.

'Take it easy on her,' my father said.

I stood in the bright light of the living-room lamp, forming a triangle with my parents on the couch and the TV. A hole opened inside of me that I wanted to fill with my mother's sadness, with my guilt, and with Nana's special power for calling attention to one's self. I did not know how to do that, how to fill the hole. So instead, I let it grow and grow until it became bigger than me. Until I became a hole that everyone could see right through. And then disappear.

*

As an apology, I used some of the money I had saved for my move out of Florida to treat my mother to the salon. While she was getting her nails painted strawberry jam, she passed out.

If it weren't for that minor gaffe, that single snafu in an otherwise impeccable performance, no one would have known the truth. Only because the stylist called for an ambulance, which took my mother to a hospital, did we discover the reality she had been hiding. The doctor explained to us that her sugar levels had risen so high, in such a short amount of time, she had nearly gone into a coma. He kept repeating how lucky we all were. *Lucky*. My mother stared at the painting of orange groves across the doctor's office. During the entire consultation, she remained silent and refrained from taking a single look at my father, me, or the doctor.

'Last year, she was diagnosed as having type-2 diabetes,' the doctor said with an obvious look of concern. 'She should not have eaten whatever pushed her blood-sugar level through the roof.'

My father and I stood like blocks of ice. A shiver passed through me. My bones became glaciers. I knew the same was true for my father because he cast a glance at me, and in his eyes, I recognized a desperate call for help.

The doctor looked at my mother, who continued to stare at those orange groves, slathered on the canvas in globs of paint.

'Does your family know you are diabetic?' the doctor asked. His frustration became more noticeable. His brow pinched his round glasses against the bridge of his square nose. He pursed his lips.

'I could sue you for sharing my private information without my consent,' my mother said.

Her voice was too soft to be taken as a serious threat. The doctor responded, 'Let's first get your blood-sugar levels under control, then we'll discuss litigation.'

As soon as we arrived home, my mother asked me if I wanted to watch *Just Like Heaven*. She acted like we had just gotten home from dinner or a day at the beach. The past twenty-four hours never happened. *Ta-Da*!

'Why would you keep diabetes a secret?' my stubborn self asked, knowing very well I could not supplicate an answer from anyone in this family simply by asking. Either as a concession or as a consolation, I do not know, I turned on the DVD player and looked for the movie.

'Don't make today any more trouble than it's already been,' she said.

My father leaned against the kitchen counter and stared at her, trying to figure something out – the formula that could crack her code. Not even his mathematical mind could calculate my mother's cryptic behavior. My mother stood in the center of the tiled kitchen, the counter angled in front of her like a podium, the wall between performer and audience. The soft ceiling lights centered on her as she stood with the bag of popcorn in her hand, its bottom edges frayed. She stared at me and in her wide-open eyes I recognized Nana, the way she looked into me so that we understood each other without words. It was her way of telling me to play along. *Show time!* And now my mother's eyes had the green emptiness that somehow filled me with memories.

'I'm not watching *Just Like Heaven*,' I said.

I found *Eternal Sunshine of the Spotless Mind* and loaded the DVD player.

As I expected, my mother complained. She reminded me that she hated tragedies. 'I want to laugh and feel good. I don't want to think about all the bad things in life.'

Still, she popped the popcorn and watched the movie. My father gave up calculating and returned to his office to compute the numbers that made sense to him. Meanwhile, I watched my mother as she dozed in and out of sleep, the TV's glow weighing on her eyelids. I tried imagining what she felt moments before she passed out: the white fluorescent lights blurring her vision. The sky pouring down powdered sugar.

The chemical smell of nail polish plugging her nose and making her swollen eyes water. How long did she plan on casting this illusion? When did she think we would realize the trick?

After we finished the popcorn, I held onto the bowl. I was afraid of getting up, of letting her out of my sight. Troubled both by a haunting familiarity and a painfully strange newness, I had to see what she was up to.

X

The week before I moved to Alaska, I visited Nana at Spring Hills. She was drawing a picture in her memory book, sitting at her table where shadow and light formed a clear border. The sun shone in from the window onto her drawing but left her in the dark.

I sat next to her, in the shadow, and held her hand to stop her. The drawing was nothing but interconnected spirals. By that time, she had grayed. It wasn't just the amount of color her face lost; it was a graying that stemmed from some place inside. Her breaths weakened. Her heart missed beats. Near her, I detected the sour odor of excess human breath. That bedroom with poor ventilation had its air dominated by carbon dioxide – the odor of those at the ends of their lives.

She apologized for leaving Cuba. 'We should have stayed with our families,' she said. When I told her I wasn't Manny, she said, 'I'm not an idiot. You're Tito-my-love.'

I did not know how long either of us had. The more I hid away and read, however, the more I thought I understood. I thought I could save us both. I held Nana and dreamed with her.

Her brittle hair had the gray in it, too, a color as thin as autumn's first frost. She leaned against me with her arms by her side. I went along with whatever memory she evoked. When she remembered an event that pre-dated my birth, I invented details to keep the dream going. And when I couldn't know a particular memory, I imagined myself there.

'You are on track to becoming *un gran ilusionista*. It doesn't matter who disappears first.' Her voice had a rare quality to it – playful, reminiscent of the days when she asked the Burger King attendant for a 'fucking napkin'.

'I can tell you what you need to know,' she said and stood up. She appeared so light, like her red and white dress kept her afloat. 'Take me to Gatorland.'

'What are we going to see at that tacky tourist trap?'

'Birds.'

I reminded her that Gatorland was known for its gators, not birds, but she insisted. If this had been a memory she dreamed, I wouldn't have known. It didn't matter one way or the other. If she could have exhumed a single shard of memory that pertained to reversing illusions, I would have been grateful.

While I drove, she complained that my parents moved to Orlando without telling her. Only because we were going somewhere by her request, and because I hoped she could keep her mind focused on that goal, I reminded her that she already lived in Orlando, and that my parents hadn't moved anywhere in almost a decade.

I hated speaking to Nana this way – all facts, like she was already dead.

The stoplight up ahead backed up the traffic. We had been waiting for several minutes.

'Facts don't matter,' Nana said. 'You must have vision.'

I closed my eyes and tried.

XI

Just a couple days after our Gatorland excursion, Nana died, on a day that was too sunny for death. The sky was dusted a powder blue. Nana's nurse had called my mother to inform her that Nana's memory had become very fragile. They were calling in hospice. When we arrived, staff explained to my mother the logistics of caring for 'the body' once she passed. I headed directly for Nana's room. The nurse, a broad-shouldered Haitian whose strong voice still had the sibilance of sympathy, suggested I brace myself. 'Are you ready?' she asked. I lied and said I was.

When I entered and saw her lying in bed, my chest became glass.

'I love you, Nana.'

'Eh? Who are you?' Her gray hair didn't even seem attached to her head, like one gust could blow it off, as if it were nothing more than accumulated dust. Her vacant eyes searched the room and then, as if she saw nothing worth the focus, closed in a painfully slow blink. When they opened once again, I saw a flash of emerald green, of hazel, of Nana.

'It's me. Tito-your-love.'

'Who?'

'Tito.'

'Who?'

'Your protégé? I don't know.'

'Who?'

'The next *gran ilusionista* who will continue your legacy!'

'Who?'

By now I was crying and couldn't continue playing her game, our final one. The air went thin like the world stopped breathing. The light came in through the window in splotches. I held Nana's hand and it felt like I was holding a pile of fine white sand. When I could keep my heart steady long enough to do so, I said goodbye.

Suddenly, as if in a glimpse of clarity that shattered the room's dense fog, a breath of a gesture that may or may not have actually happened, Nana said, 'The real magic is when Pepe returns.' It felt like I stood there for hours – crying, laughing, crying some more. In just a couple of days, I would leave home. Disappear so I wouldn't disappear, so to speak. Quietly slip into exile, like it was my turn to tell Nana's story. The one without an ending. And yet, with her last words, she gave away the plot twist. Of course, I wouldn't realize any of this until much later. A lifetime passed. It could have been hours or minutes. By the time Nana was gone, I could have been anywhere.

Most recently, in Alaska, I was woken at 4am not by Nana's spirit but by my ringing cell phone. It was my father calling. When I answered, I forgot that in Florida it was 8am and asked what he was doing awake in the middle of the night.

'I haven't slept in two days,' he said. 'Your mother brought home a pack of store-bought cupcakes.'

'How many did she eat?'

'All of them.'

His words were boulders forming a rockslide. I felt the weight of his worry, his panic. He wasn't just informing me of my mother's disregard for her diabetes, he was pleading with me.

'It's like she's trying to eat herself to death. Her blood-sugar level is above 300.'

'What should I do?' I asked. Some nights I had to strap myself onto my bed to keep from floating away into the night. I'd lost more weight, lost several inches of height. Strong winds, whipping down from the tall mountain wall on the east side of the city, lifted me off my feet. I had to grab ahold of trees to stay grounded. There wasn't much I could do.

My father breathed into the phone, as if to show his regret at what he was about to say. 'She wants to see you.'

'There isn't much to see.'

'I don't know how it all works, Tito. It's been years since you've been home and your mother acts like you're still here. She's kept your room exactly how you left it.'

He released a long sigh into the phone and I felt his breath against my cheek. My father rarely made requests from people. This was hard for him, I knew. I sat up in my bed and felt the chill of night prick my skin. Spring had just started breaking winter. Sunlight leaked into the sky, giving it that ghost-skin blue that would soon last the entire night here.

'Look,' my father said, his voice a little less agitated, 'you're not the one who's disappearing. You chose to live four thousand, seven hundred, and twelve miles away. You can cast your life anyway you want. If you want to fly around the world all alone, nobody can stop you. But at least let yourself exist once in a while. Don't become one of the forgotten.'

I hung up.

For a while, I stared at my phone, expecting my father to call back. He didn't.

I loosened the leash strapping me to my bed and floated into the living room. Fingers of purple light reached in from the windows. The cold carpet crunched under my feet. I turned on the TV. The light radiating from the screen instantly warmed the living room.

In a climactic moment, an unloved middle sister was screaming for help because the kitchen was on fire.

Of course, the entire gang arrived. Uncle, younger sister, older sister, and father all threw cups of water into the oven until the flames subsided. The smoke cleared and the flat, shadowless light of the sitcom household was restored. But I knew the smoke was still there. I could smell it. Whatever the unloved middle sister was baking had the odor of burnt leg hair. It was awful. It only cleared on the surface because that's all anyone cares about.

'What in the world were you doing?' the responsible father asked.

'No one likes me because I'm the middle child,' the middle child said. 'So I wanted to impress everyone by making a combination of everyone's favorite pie. Uncle loves peanut butter, big sis likes rhubarb, little sis likes baby food, and you like mince.'

'Honey,' Father said in his trademark father voice, all impossible love and patience. He got down on one knee to be eye level with his unloved daughter. The rest of the gang gathered around, leaning on each other like the perfect family. 'The middle child also has an important role in this show.'

'I do?' she asked.

'Let me give you a few last words from Erasmus's *Folly*. If someone should try to strip away the costumes and make-up from the actors performing a play on the stage and to display them to the spectators in their own natural appearance, wouldn't he ruin the whole play? Wouldn't all the spectators be right to throw rocks at such a madman and drive him out of the theater? This deception, this disguise, is the very thing that holds the attention of the spectators. Now the whole life of mortal men, what is it but a sort of play, in which various persons make their entrances in various costumes, and each one plays his own part until the director gives him his cue to leave the stage? True, all these images are unreal, but this play cannot be performed in any other way.'

Middle sister smiled and kissed Father's cheek. Then everyone embraced in one big hug.

In a single motion, I picked up the coffee table in the living room and flung it at the TV. The screen blurred, cracked, then zipped into silence. With the room no longer illuminated by the TV, twilight clawed the walls. I slammed the TV screen down onto the floor, as if I were afraid that a broken screen wasn't enough to stop its images. I couldn't stand the illusion any longer. I had done everything in my power to reverse the spell. I reversed my entire life, from tropics to arctic, from drunk to sober, from sunlight to darkness. I couldn't tell if moving to Alaska counted as a reversal. Was my retreat north just another stage of my illusion, as Titi suggested?

I had to focus. My heart jumped into my throat and I felt dizzy. I had to know what was real. No more ghosts. No more stages.

I pushed over my bookcase. The wood split when it landed so that books spilled out like blood. I grabbed them at random and tore out pages. They had to be destroyed. I couldn't be misled anymore.

Nana was gone. My mother was now sick. Dane's mother was probably dead. And I was the one uncertain if I even existed.

Pages fell like snow in my living room. The air smelled like wisdom. I was dubious. I grabbed *The Waste Land* and tore the entire binding. Rustling pages filled my apartment. I tore out more and more until I saw Nana's red shawl. I turned to face her, standing amidst the falling pages. Each sheet passed through her, spiraling into and out of her body. She looked regal, alive. It was like she was all flesh, warm and present. I wanted to curl up on her lap and have her play the organ into my spine. I wanted to go wherever her spirit went when she disappeared. I wanted to give up.

Nana pointed down to where I was sitting. Her gesture somehow stirred the paper that had already settled on the floor. An updraft sent them soaring once again. They slapped against each other and crinkled as they looped around in the air. I looked to where Nana was pointing and found a thin, yellow slip of paper. For a moment, I stared at it without moving, listening to the ruffle of paper around me. It felt like a trap, like another illusion. It wasn't – couldn't be – another note from Manny. I glanced around me, as if he were in my living room, too, and had just placed that note. Nana was now gone, again. There were only torn pages flitting in the shrinking light, casting ribbons of shadows.

I picked up the note and opened it. As the paper unfolded, I felt the permanence that always accompanied my grandfather's notes. I knew it would be the last because I could almost guess what it was going to say. I knew that, once I returned to Florida, I would no longer wake up to Nana's spirit. There would only be the darkness of an empty room, with only my breathing to fill it.

Todo el mundo desaparece. Lo real magia es permenecer visible. The world will disappear. The real magic is to remain visible.

I called my father back.

'Are you still there?' he answered the phone, straight up, without the slightest surprise.

'I'm coming home,' I told him.

'We'll leave the window open,' he said.

I wondered if he'd known all along.

*

I paid for Nana's and my admission at Gatorland. After stepping out onto the zigzagging boardwalks that crossed swamps of hissing gators, the sunlight bleached Nana's face, made her appear dreamlike. Already she had developed a ghostly quality.

'You must have vision,' she reminded me. 'See things as they really are.'

As the planks creaked underneath our steps, Nana repeated how much she loved coming here to see the birds.

'Where are you moving?' she asked.

'Alaska.'

'Then you have to see the birds.'

Below us, a sprawling net of coarse reptilian skin pulsed menacingly. Beads of yellow eyes watched us. The occasional open jaw revealed rows of deadly teeth. Really, despite the prima facie threat of an alligator, the fact that they were confined in such crowded spaces aroused more pity than fear. If you stared into those yellow eyes, you'd recognize dejection more than an urge to kill. We followed a bridge through dense palmetto that infused the humid air with a pleasant aroma of pine. Nana stopped suddenly and held onto the wood railing. She held her heart, as if keeping it in place, and panted. Her eyes searched the enmeshed trees as her face gasped in confusion. For a moment, she seemed completely lost, unable to recognize anything.

'I'm out of breath,' she finally said, twisting her mouth the way she did when she tasted something bad.

I held her shoulders and looked around. No one was near. There wasn't a single so-called 'ranger' patrolling the boardwalks. I considered calling out for help, despite still finding it hard to believe that Nana's old age, her deteriorating health and mind weren't aspects of another act that she had under complete control. Panic tightened my muscles, knotted my vocal cords.

After a few seconds, Nana swallowed hard and said, 'The tower is up ahead. We can see the birds there.' She resumed walking and, still holding onto her, I followed.

'Who comes to Gatorland to see birds?'

'Who goes anywhere to see anything?' She smiled, letting me know she felt fine.

As a white observation tower came into view through the arching palms, Nana recounted all the times she came here as a child.

'You didn't come to Orlando until late in your life,' I reminded her.

'Now you sound like your mother,' she protested, like a child told not to play.

Before we started up the tower, I asked Nana if she was okay taking all those stairs. She looked at me, and in her hazel eyes were years of longing, the signal that she was back to normal. '*Mi madre*,' she said, scoffed, and led me up the spiraling staircase.

At the top, we had a view of the entire park. Layers of green upon green. The wet ground slithered with ancient bodies the same color as the trees itching in the sticky breeze. I thought of the pond near the house, where I spent the first couple of years after moving to Orlando, baiting a reptile to attack me. They had refused a role in my drama.

Nana pointed to a nearby bough, on which sat a roseate spoonbill in brilliant evening pink feathers. It pointed back with its long, black-tipped beak. Nana and the bird stared at each other as if silently conversing. Nana pointed in a new direction, towards a duo of wood stork, their white puffy bodies guarding an impressive nest. Again, they locked stares with Nana, their gray withered faces entranced. It was as if the birds appeared only when Nana pointed. They existed for her, by her. The only reason I could bear witness was my being here, standing next to Nana.

'How do you do it?'

Nana wore a content expression, as if everything in her life fit perfectly together like the individual straws making the stork's nest. The bright sunlight unfiltered by a cloudless blue sky changed the color of her eyes from hazel to mauve to gray – to Gatorland green.

'I remember when your mother wanted to go study dance in Russia,' she said.

'Did she go?'

'Out of nowhere I started having heart palpitations.' Nana winked. 'She had to stay and take care of me.'

She pointed again towards a bare stump of a pine tree, where a great egret danced. Its long neck sprang soft curves as its wings blurred its body. The reflection of the sun on its white feathers made it glow like a new star.

'It's like San Lázaro,' she said in a voice reserved for prayer, songlike. 'He's the most popular in Cuba. In December, you see people limping on the streets, held up by crutches, cigars dangling in their mouths. San Lázaro represents illness, and yet is the most beloved. The dead become more alive.'

The great egret took flight and soared over our heads. As it did so, Nana applauded, amused by her own show. She was always the first audience.

I didn't want to ruin the moment. I wanted to believe. As much as it worried me how Nana would respond, I couldn't help telling her, 'Mom's taking insulin now.'

At first Nana's eyes went blank, losing her emerald focus. When they returned to hazel she said, 'My daughter has her tricks, too.'

'I don't think they're tricks.' The late spring heat and unfettered sunshine could not keep me from shivering. The sweat dripping down my back felt like ice.

'*No me digas.*'

'I feel like I'm going crazy,' I said. 'No one can remember anything the way it happened. I need to go far, far away. I want cold weather, mountains, a landscape completely opposite this one.'

'*Dimelo en Español.*'

In Spanish, I told Nana that only the extreme opposite could distinguish reality from illusion. I explained that I wasn't simply running away. I was trying to discover my own life.

'*Ay*, don't play tricks on your mother.'

'I'll take care of Mom if things get really bad, but I need to get far away from the stage. Being here requires too much pretending. We spend so much energy burying secrets everyone already knows.'

A sudden rush of guilt made me want to end the conversation. It didn't feel right burdening Nana with this information. I thought maybe she would have an answer. As if she could influence illusions cast by other people. If that were true, of course, she would have been able to reverse my steady disappearance. I looked out at the swamps, the green mess of land, but couldn't spot one single bird, not like when Nana pointed. In every direction the horizon remained grounded, not a hint of flight.

'*No te vayas*,' she said. 'It's not right for a mother to lose her child.'

'Would things be different now if you had let Mom go to Russia?'

'In Spanish.'

'*¿Qué pasa si mamá fue a Rusia?*'

'You wouldn't exist,' she said.

Quite possibly. My mother probably wouldn't have married my father. Who knows if she would have returned to the United States? To her last days, Nana retained the ability to enter moments of clarity so sharp that what she said could only be called wisdom.

She held my arm and smiled as her eyes watered with a warmness that felt like nostalgia. The firmness of her grip, despite the frailty of her hand, calmed me. Memories of her apartment in Miami, with the plastic plants lining every shelf, windowsill, and table, and of the taste of mamey filled my mind. Nana pointed somewhere beyond the observation tower, this time to no distinct location.

'Which one do you think is Pepe?' she asked, but there were no birds to be seen.

Then, the instant she lowered her pointing finger and held onto the railing, it was as if the sky exploded into little shards of frenetic life, each piece spiraling above us, birds of flight forming their own galaxy. Rising up from the palms, lake, and pines were all sorts of species. Tricolored herons, blue herons, green herons, and night herons swirled around the observation deck. Ospreys perched on the railings, flapping their wings and whistling in unison out to the universe. Limpkins rocketed upwards and then dived down in a continual undulation. Swallow-tailed kites soared in zigzags as if mocking the layout of boardwalks stuck on the ground. Waves of anhingas, cormorants, and bitterns glided with sprawled wings that eclipsed the sun and refracted its light into thousands of dazzling rays. Red-shouldered hawks left streaming ribbons of air in their wingtip vortices that circled around the tower. And, at the center of the impossible allelomimesis, drawing little circles high up above, around which the flocking murmuration performed, were three purple-tipped nightingales.

Also in the Fairlight Moderns series

Book club and writers' circle notes for the
Fairlight Moderns can be found at
www.fairlightmoderns.com

Share your thoughts about the book
with #TakingFlightNovella